I0684326

Bitterroot Flowers

Nez Perce Coven Chronicles Book 3

By Lorretta Smith

Star Sapphire Press
Darby, Montana
2019

First edition
First printing 2019
Book design by Lorretta Smith Cover art by Lorretta Smith
Author photo by Renee Knowles

Library of Congress Cataloging in Publication Data Smith, Lorretta 1972- Bitterroot Flowers/ Nez Perce Coven Chronicles / Lorretta Smith -- 1st ed. ISBN: 978-1-7337656-2-6   Library of Congress Control Number: 2019913733 Star Sapphire Printing / Star Sapphire Press
629 Bridge Lane
Darby, Mt 59829
Printed in the United States of America

Born and raised all over the Northwest, Lorretta makes her home in Darby, Montana where she lives with her two pugs, Lollah Loo and Corona Cerveza, and her Maine Coon Cat, Clyde. They live in the tiny house she built herself on the banks of the Bitterroot River. When she isn't writing, Lorretta enjoys camping, hiking, rafting and kayaking.

Lorretta is divorced with one child, twenty-one year old son, Cory, who is the love of her life, partner in adventures and comic relief in life. Lorretta looks forward to planning adventures with her new grandson, Braxton. She earned a Bachelors degree from Eastern New Mexico University in Psychology and Sociology. Prior to her writing career, Lorretta worked as a social worker.

Photo by Renee Knowles

Dedication

To my new, and first, grandson, Braxton. I can't wait to take you on many adventures!

1

I choked on my donut as the long, lean, sexy Were cat slinked through the door, gliding like pudding slipping off a spoon. He shot me a come-hither grin. Mmm. I wanted to hitherly come. "Shy de la Angelino, beautiful as ever."

Running my tongue along my top lip, "Devon Ballantine. What brings you to this side of the mountain?" I rose to my feet, extending my right arm in greeting. We clasped hands, similar to an arm-wrestling hold, common greeting among Weres. His sexy lips pressed a kiss on the back of my knuckles. His eyes widened as my mini kachina familiar peeked out from under my hair. "This is Dokwl," I explained, nodding towards him.

The smile slid from his face and stress marred his handsome features. He reached a finger to Dokwl. Dokwl grasped it with both of his hands, in way of greeting. Tucking a lock of his long blond hair behind his ear, Devon replied, "I'm actually here regarding your professional skills, rather than that dinner you owe me."

Laughing, I raised an eyebrow inquiringly. Ryan cleared his throat as he entered behind Devon. My boss and boyfriend, Malachi's father. He walked around the table, taking a seat at the head.

"Can I get you a beverage? Tea, coffee, cappuccino, pop?" Dylan offered, following his father into the conference room. Strolling over to the complicated machine in the corner, he turned towards Devon.

"I'll take coffee, thanks."

"What's up?" I asked sipping my chai tea. My professional capacity pertained to my employment at 3D Investigations. The three D's referred to Ryan, Dylan and Malachi. I was their witch for hire. We investigated incidents magical in nature, both privately and contracting with local law enforcement. Devon and I sorta have a history. He negotiated an arranged marriage with my deranged grandfather for my hand. I told my grandfather where to put the arrangement and told Devon to call me. He was hot. What can I say?

Devon melted into a mocha leather chair at the cherry wood table, across from me. His gaze wandered out to the Salmon River flowing by our office. Sighing deeply, "Four women from my Pack disappeared over the last six weeks."

"Oh, fuck." Dylan whispered, inhaling sharply as the coffee percolated. Dokwl climbed down from his perch under my hair, standing beside my mug of tea.

I shot Dylan a grimacing look. "Were the women in their teens, early twenties?" I tried to keep my voice flat, no emotion, as dread grew in the pit of my stomach.

Devon thought for a moment. "Yeah." Then he added, "They all lived alone."

"Didn't you receive a notice from the Were Council? About a witch who preys upon Were women?" I questioned, leaning back in my chair. "The Regional Alpha should have sent notification several months ago."

He looked at me, astounded. "Noooo."

Dylan handed him a coffee. He held out a tiny cup for Dokwl. The little Kachina insisted on drinking his own cappuccino when everyone else ordered one. Dylan pushed a few buttons on the machine, starting his beverage.

Sighing, "We investigated a situation about six months ago where members of a coven here in Lewiston / Clarkston were kidnapping Weres, mostly women. One of the witches imprisoned and tortured them. He escaped from jail about four months ago. Malachi and I informed the Regional Alpha regarding the risk he posed and recommended all prides and packs be apprised."

"Before we jump on that wagon, what did the women look like? Thin, long dark hair, attractive?" Ryan questioned from his seat at the head of the table, sipping his coffee as Dylan took a seat, sipping a cappuccino.

Devon nodded. Abruptly, I stood up, stalking to the French doors, staring out at the water flowing by. I pulled my phone from the back pocket of my jeans, immediately dialing my uncle, Alberto, leader of our coven. He answered after only a few bars of Chopin played in my ear.

"Hey, Kitten. What's up?" He responded, with a smile in his voice.

"Devon Ballantine, Heir Apparent to the Bitterroot River Pack informed us at 3D Investigations that he's missing four women."

"Oh, shit." Alberto paused for a moment, "I hoped he moved to another region of the world. I'll call your cousins, Lance and Tristan. The three of you go and perform a preliminary investigation and report back to me immediately. If you verify it's Scott Clark, we'll send reinforcements. I'll call Stephen Kane and provide him with a head's up." He ended the call, abruptly.

I turned back to face the men at the table, inhaling deeply. "My uncle authorized my cousins and I to determine if this is related to the previous case we investigated," I informed them.

"Dylan, accompany them and provide any and all support required," Ryan stated, begrudgingly.

"My pack will cover the costs associated with the investigation. We protect and care for our own," Devon replied. "You're all welcome to stay at the clan home while working on our situation."

"Give us twenty minutes to gear up and make arrangements, then we'll teleport to the clan home. If you like, I'll 'port you as well," I offered, smiling.

Nodding, "I like. Let me tell my driver to head on back. Then, we can 'port to your Pride home and then to mine. Hell, set up a portal. Easy travel back and forth would be perfect," Devon offered with another sexy smile.

"I don't know if Malachi would approve." Ryan stated disdainfully, attempting to remind me I already had a boyfriend. Ryan wasn't a Were. He failed to understand the polyamorous tendencies within our species.

Devon snickered. "He's on tour. He's not around." Shooting me a heart stopping smile, spreading his arms wide, "Me, on the other hand, am here and eager to meet your every need."

Rolling my eyes, "It's my house. Devon, go talk to your driver. Dylan, meet us at the lodge," I stated as my phone made cricket noises. Uncle Alberto. I answered it.

"Kane wants to send his son Nathaniel, as a representative of the Orchards Coven." Scott Clark used to be a member of the Orchards Coven, his father, the leader, prior to their arrests for kidnapping, murder and other heinous crimes. "Absolutely, under no circumstances, allow Nate to get hurt on this excursion. The last thing we need is incur the wrath of another Coven."

I nodded, totally agreeing, even though he couldn't see, "Tell him to pack a bag. Devon invited us to stay at the Pride home. Have Lance and Tristan grab him and meet at my lodge. We'll 'port together to the Bitterroot Valley."

Devon reentered the conference room as I hung up the call. "The Orchards Coven is sending a representative. Prior to his arrest, Scott Clark belonged to their coven," I explained. Hastily, I rinsed out my mug, leaving it in the drainer to dry. Dokwl jumped into the sink, careful of the splashing water, rinsing his cup as well. He leaped into the drainer, setting his next to mine. I rolled my eyes.

"I'm heading home to pack and will meet at the lodge in ten minutes," Dylan announced. "I'll check in regularly, Dad." He nodded to Devon and me as he exited the room, heading to the portal I created to their house and my lodge from the office to make teleporting easier.

"And we're heading to my lodge. I need to pack as well and take care of a few things. I'll tell Shay to come in to cover the office while I'm away," I informed Ryan. I held a hand out to Dokwl. He jumped onto it, ran up my arm and tucked under my hair.

He hesitated, then stated, "Be safe."

"Devon, you're with me. Let's head to the lodge."

Shooting me a smile holding the properties to melt chocolate in Siberia, "I'd follow you to hell. And enjoy it," Devon replied, wickedly, waggling his eyebrows at me.

Again, I rolled my eyes. At least I possessed some immunity to his charms. He followed me through the office and into the library which led to the courtyard. A large blue spruce tree dominated the area. Attached to the tree lay the portals. I'm a witch. Earth is my primary element, water secondary. Oh, yeah, and I'm a Were Bobcat. Alpha Female. Which means I don't take shit from anyone.

2

Within twenty minutes, everyone met up at the Salmon River Pride home, a cedar log lodge resting at the confluence of the Snake and Salmon Rivers. I found it in a neglected and run-down state about six months ago. We worked to rebuild the lodge to its past glory. Tristan and Lance each claimed a room and were upstairs packing. I left Devon with my sister, Shay, and Rhiannon, a werewolf who joined our pride after we freed her from Clark's evil laboratory.

My bedroom faced the Salmon River. With the French doors open, the flowing water provided the soundtrack to the rugged wilderness landscape. I quickly packed a bag, throwing in jeans, sweaters and unmentionables. Devon's pack home lay within the Bitterroot Mountains, South of Darby, Montana. In early fall, the temperatures tended to be colder than we were accustomed to within the canyon walls protecting the Salmon River. I felt Dylan's arrival at the lodge as he came through the portal. I finished packing and raced back downstairs. Tristan, Lance and Nate stood in the library listening as Devon brought them up to speed. He shot me a sexy smile. Dylan and Shay whispered together by the bar, smiling at each other. Their relationship moved at the speed of a glacier. Malachi and I, on the other hand, surrendered to intense animal magnetism quicker than water flows downhill.

Shay and I are identical twins. But we use glamour spells to differentiate between us. My hair tends to be copper with gold highlights while Shay chooses gold with copper highlights. Her eyes twinkle bluish green while mine are greenish blue. She's cautious, studious and thinks before she acts. I take running leaps off cliffs blindfolded, usually with no prior warning to anyone and no safety net below.

"Before we leave, let me give you a head's up regarding the," Devon paused, searching for the correct term, "sleeping arrangements at our Pride home. We maintain three communal rooms. The Vanilla room provides a," again he hesitated, "normal sexual experience. One on one, missionary, doggy style, sixty-nine, hetero, homo. The Pralines and Cream room allows for mild to moderate BDSM, ménage à trois, toys, etc. If you desire hard core BDSM, the Rocky Road room delivers all you imagine. Each room requires complete voluntary participation. Voyeurism is okay. If you prefer a private room, the third floor provides a variety. If the door's open, the room is available."

A wide smile flashed across Lance and Tristan's faces. "I love the free love philosophy of Were clans," Tristan announced.

"Completely agree," Lance responded, nodding enthusiastically.

I glanced towards Nate. He appeared a little surprised. To allay inter coven relations, I decided to call his dad to ensure the sleeping arrangements met with his approval. Unsure how old Nate was, I guessed somewhere in his late teens, maybe twenty.

"Shy, I'll escort you to any room you want, my private room or will prepare a room to fit your needs," Devon offered, magnanimously, with a heart stopping sexy smile.

Laughing at his unabashed flirting, "Thanks, I need to make a call first. Then, let's discuss the details of your missing women," I suggested, gazing into the promises his eyes held for me.

Shooting me a sardonic look, "You aren't calling Malachi," Devon ordered flatly.

I shook my head, scoffing. "We reached an understanding when we're separated. He's a strong proponent of an open relationship. Especially when on tour." I shared. "I'm calling Nate's dad. I don't want his coven angry with ours over something like this. We grew up surrounded by Were life and know what to expect. Though rooms named after ice cream proved a new twist for me."

"Aw, Shy. He's young and good looking. He'll be fine. We promise to take good care of him," Tristan offered, slinging an arm around Nate's shoulders, ruffling his hair.

"Every young person needs the experience of a Were clan home," Lance added. "It's a right of passage for every teenager, male, female, gay, straight. The perfect place to try … new ideas with no recriminations."

I rolled my eyes, pulled my phone out of my back pocket and found Steve Kane in my contact list. He picked up on the first ring.

"What's up, Shyenne?" Steve asked.

"So, we intend to stay at the Were Pride home in Montana. We need to conserve as much magical energy as possible and don't want to be 'porting back and forth," I began.

"That makes complete sense, if this is Clark, you'll need all the magic you can muster."

I hesitated, "Are you… familiar with the … lack of … uh… the un-inhibited sexual activity typical in Were Clan homes?" Normally, I'm not very politically correct, so this conversation proved difficult for me. Insulting a coven leader would be a bad thing.

Steve laughed. "My fondest memories growing up include staying in a Were Pack home for a week, as a teenager. Nate will be fine. Good experience for him."

Sighing with relief, "Lance and Tristan said they'd watch out for him."

He laughed again. "Update me when you know who we're dealing with." He hung up.

I walked back to the men, gave them a thumbs up. "Steve's cool with it."

"Get a couple beers in my dad and he'll tell you about the week he spent in a Wolf Pack home when he was sixteen," Nate smirked.

"Great. Now that we all know we are getting laid tonight, lets figure out what's going on." I suggested. "Let's 'port to the Bitterroot and get started."

We walked out the French doors to a large bull pine tree standing next to the Snake River.

"How do we do this 'porting thing?" Devon asked.

"Picture in your head your home. Picture a pine tree close to it. It's easiest for us to port through trees." I explained. I placed my left hand on the trunk of our tree.

Devon looked surprised. "Trees? Seriously?"

Dokwl poked out from under my hair, nodding. "Trees provide the foundation for life. Oxygen." He explained in his tiny, tinny voice.

Smiling, "I believe astral space is comprised of the essence from trees. Teleporting between the same species of trees simplifies the process for us."

Nodding in understanding, "I'll take your word for it," Devon smirked, winking.

I checked his mind for his house and pine tree. He imagined me naked, against said pine. Smacking him playfully in the arm, "Just the pine tree, please."

Astonished, he laughed. "You saw that?" In his mind, he removed me from the image, leaving just the pine tree in a wave of green lawn.

With one hand on the tree at my lodge, I dug my bare feet into the dry green grass, curling my toes into the rich soil. I reached for Devon with my other arm. He walked into my embrace. His thighs pressed into mine, my breasts crushed to his chest as his cock rubbed against me. I looked up into his eyes, dark blue, the color of a Montana sky. His lips brushed against me as I melded us into the tree. We sank into the earth and flowed along with the essence of trees, soil, earth. Moving through rock, mountains, streams, rivers, our beings glided from one forest to the next.

We emerged next to a Ponderosa Pine. My bare toes dug into frost covered grass. Wind nipped into my cheek as I became aware of our surroundings. Devon's warm breath blew against my lips. "Open your eyes."

I was right. His eyes totally matched a Montana sky. The deep, dark blue irises gazed into mine.

"Wow! It's freaking cold!" Tristan exclaimed as he stood next to me

9

with Nate. Lance and Dylan appeared around the tree.

"This is beautiful!" Nate commented, as he observed our new locale.

Breaking away from Devon's eyes, I glanced around at the surroundings. We appeared in the backyard behind a stone and log house. Thick grass covered a football field sized backyard. A twenty person hot tub lay by sliding glass doors with a huge outdoor oven and barbecue opposite. An oversized picnic table stood between the tub and outdoor kitchen. Adjacent to the kitchen, a full bar seating six faced the cooking area.

Leading the way, Devon entered through the sliding glass doors into a massive great room. Assorted couches, recliners and easy chairs littered the room with a bar and bar stools taking up a corner. The largest television I ever saw completely dominated a wall and the room.

"Dude, Monday Night Football is at your house! I'll bring Taco Bell!" Tristan declared.

"Totally! That is awesome!" Lance gazed in wonder at the tv.

Dokwl performed a series of flips, landing on the back of the couch, cheering. He loved television. He didn't care what we watched, he enjoyed the big picture and sounds.

Devon smiled, widely. "We do love our football. With surround sound, it's like we're in the stadium, except more comfortable. And warmer."

"We're definitely doing football season here. Honestly, the girls just don't understand." Dylan stated, shaking his head, sadly, then flashed a smile towards me.

"We'd love it if you guys did the football thing here rather than our house," I rolled my eyes, realizing all the eye rolling would result in a headache in my near future.

Laughing, Devon took drink orders from everyone and sent a pretty young werewolf to fetch them, as we all found a seat. "The first woman we missed was Carly. She's a werewolf, lives in an apartment in Hamilton and works at a gas station. After five days, her landlord called me due to her rent being late. Inside her place, everything appears fine. We found her car parked behind the gas station where she works. Her cell lay underneath it.

No cameras. The gas station assumed she caught a ride with one of us. She tends to experience a lot of car trouble." Devon explained as the young lady brought our drinks over from the bar.

"Thanks, Michelle. We believe she vanished about a week before the next disappearance. The second was Dana, a mountain lion. She lives on the east side of Hamilton, in a fairly rural area. She works at Safeway. After missing three shifts, I received a call. We figure she disappeared five days before. We found her purse and cell lying on the kitchen counter at her home.

"The third lives just outside Darby, Chrissy, leopard. She bartends at the casino. Near as I can tell, she disappeared four days after Dana vanished. A neighbor called me when they walked over to borrow some sugar. Her house looked like a fight broke out, broken furniture, plants knocked over, shattered dishes." Devon took a swig of his Beam and Coke. "And the fourth, Melanie, another wolf, we believe went missing two days ago. I received notification last night. She lives up by Sula. Her place appeared completely trashed. She bartends at the Rocky Knob."

"You're the emergency contact for all your people?" Lance asked as he reclined back on the couch.

Shaking his head, Devon answered. "Only for those who don't know anyone locally. We maintain a significant presence online and offer shelter to any Were. We assist them with finding employment, housing, pursuing their education, whatever needs they express. Two of the ladies came to us locally, estranged from their families, and two we met online and helped them to relocate here."

"They all interacted with the public through their employment," Tristan noted.

"The disappearances occurred closer together and became more physical towards the last," Dylan observed.

"Initially, he took the women in public places, then he followed them home." I tried to keep my outward appearance professionally calm, but inside, I cringed. I picked up on the significant escalation of violence, as well.

"We need to observe all the scenes, as soon as possible. If the abductor used magic, we'll pick up on it."

Devon glanced at his watch. "Do you want to start with the first abduction or the closest?"

Hesitating for a moment, "Let's investigate chronologically. I'm concerned with the progression of violence and the time periods decreasing between the disappearances." I decided, reaching my feet. "That doesn't bode well for his psychopathology." I'd watched enough forensic television shows to know it was an indication of a serial killer suffering a meltdown.

"Do you want to drive or 'port? Carly's abduction occurred about forty miles from here," Devon asked. He stood up and walked over to a hutch. Opening a cabinet, rows of keys hung from labeled hooks. He picked a set.

"We probably won't glean much from Carly's site as it happened in a public parking lot. But, the second victim," Tristan looked down at his notes, "Dana, lives in Hamilton, too. I think it's imperative to discern the differences between her abduction site and the other two victims."

"How does that pertain to 'porting versus driving?" Lance asked, not catching Tristan's train of thought.

"How's he transporting them? Is he driving? 'Porting? I think we need to drive to the sites, observe the scene from a vehicle. Identify places enroute utilizing cameras, determine his approach to the scenes," Tristan explained.

"He 'ported when he escaped prison." Lance observed, bewildered.

"No. He used a charm." I corrected my cousin. "He may not know how to 'port yet. Not without someone teaching him. Tristan's right. We need to take a vehicle. At least, until we rule out him driving to the abduction sites."

We loaded up in a forest green Ford Excursion. The drive up the Bitterroot Valley was beautiful. The Pride home lay in the Bitterroot Mountains, about twenty miles from the small town of Darby. The road followed the west fork of the Bitterroot River. We passed fields of hay, cows, horses and even buffalo. Darby appeared like a town from the old west, with wood storefronts and hitching posts for horses. A gas station, grocery store, couple of bars, couple of churches, a candy store, a couple antique shops, several restaurants and a liquor store lined the main street, Highway ninety-three. Fifteen miles later, we reached Trapper Peak Convenience Store.

"Here's the gas station where Carly works. She parked back here behind the building." The gas station lay right on the highway. A multitude of vehicles lined up at the numerous pumps. The business advertised a deli and convenience store.

"This appears to be an incredibly busy place. It would be difficult to abduct someone here," Lance noted, confused, as he observed cars pulling out and driving in, with people entering and exiting the store.

Devon drove around the building. A single row of parking lay under two tall street lights. He pulled into a spot and we disembarked. "Here's where we found her car." He pointed to the middle spot within the row. Lance and I stood back and "searched" for remnants of magic.

"Someone cast a detect magic spell and a locate spell," I stated, glancing at Devon.

"Law enforcement, probably. I called them once I realized none of us picked her up."

"Was she a local or one of the people you chatted up on the internet?" Dylan asked, as he surveyed the parking spot.

"She came to us from Seattle. A werewolf attacked her down at Pike Market, turning her. Her family couldn't accept the change. The metamorphosis proved to be incredibly difficult for her." Devon explained. "At first, I thought she ran off. After the second and third disappearances came to light, I realized…"

A moment of silence overcame us. "Do you think we might be able to obtain a copy of the police report?" Dylan questioned.

Rocking his head side to side, Devon contemplated the question. "Law enforcement tends to be difficult to work with. I know one detective who shows a little promise. He's proven in the past to be more openminded than most, when it comes to Weres."

"Is he the witch casting the spells?" Lance asked, trying to make sense of the crime scene.

Shaking his head, "No. The sheriff's office employs a patrol officer that is a witch. They utilize her skills sparingly." Devon explained.

"She's the one we need to talk with, discover if she noticed anything specific to the magic user before she cast," Lance remarked.

"Let's check out the other victim's house here in Hamilton, prior to contacting law enforcement. We may pick up on other things to question them about," Dylan suggested.

"Did law enforcement view all of the scenes?" I asked, hoping they had not. The witch contaminated this scene. If she cast spells at the other homes, it may prove difficult to determine Scott Clark's possible involvement.

Devon shook his head. "I called them for the second disappearance but when the third and fourth occurred right on top of the other two, I decided to call you, instead."

"Good move. We should be able to identify whether or not Clark is the perpetrator easily enough if the abduction scene is intact," Lance announced as we walked back towards the vehicle.

We loaded up in the Excursion and Devon drove to Dana's home. Not too far from the gas station, the small white clapboard house lay at the end of a long dirt road. Houses stood within sight, but trees blocked a clear view of the yard and front door.

Tristan leaned forward from the far back seat, "Stop short of the house. Let's walk up."

Exiting the vehicle, Lance and I "searched" for signs of magic. Dylan took pictures of the house and grounds while Tristan surveyed the driveway and parking area. A green Subaru was parked beside the house.

"That damn witch has no idea what the hell she's doing," Lance remarked, hands on hips, turned away disgustedly.

"Could she cast anymore fucking spells?" I asked rhetorically. We observed the remnants of a number of spells: detect, identify, locate and a failed clairvoyance. "She threw out a number of spells, hoping to find something." Walking up to the stoop, Devon pulled a key out of his pocket and unlocked the door. Inside, a couch, love seat and recliner in brown leather outfitted the tidy small living room.

I doubted it possible, but the witch cast even more spells in here. I shook my head, in disgust. It seemed pretty near impossible to discern her magic from any other caster. Between a multitude of spells and failed attempts, it would require hours to ascertain what she cast and if another witch used magics. I always assigned that job to my twin, Shaylenne. She picked magic apart. I didn't possess the virtue of patience.

Dokwl popped onto my shoulder. He surveyed the scene. "Lots of untrained magic attempted to understand what occurred here. The caster failed."

Lance nodded in agreement. "We won't learn anything. The witch completely obliterated any magical evidence that may have been present," pronounced Lance as he surveyed the little house, in disgust.

Tristan walked in the door and surveyed the room. He turned around and grasped the knob, as if answering a knock. He crumpled to the floor, then sat up, looking around. I gazed at him, raising an eyebrow. Tristan pointed to his feet, behind the door. A single floral slipper lay next to his shoe. "He hit her with a sleep spell, I think. Here, by my head, this stand has a little blood at the bottom corner where she smacked it going down. One slipper fell off her foot. I don't see the other one anywhere."

Tilting my head, I considered his theory. His scenario fit the available evidence. Nothing else seemed out of the ordinary. We performed a walk-through of the house, but found no other clues in the tidy area.

"Should we head to the Sheriff's Office?" Devon asked as we made our way back out to the car.

"No, let's hold off. If law enforcement hasn't visited the other two sites, we need to before their witch unintentionally screws everything up," Lance interjected.

"Or, we could take her along and teach her what to do so she could provide a benefit to the police," I suggested.

15

Lance rolled his eyes and Tristan laughed. "You sound just like my dad." In a deep voice with a Native American accent, "Make every moment a teaching moment." Lance groaned. Dokwl laughed aloud, slapping his knee.

3

*W*hile the rest of our group went to find drinks, Devon, Dylan and I entered the Ravalli County Sheriff's Office. Devon requested to speak with Detective Harrison through a bulletproof window. We waited on hard wooden benches before a tall, clean-shaven blond, early thirties, dressed in Wranglers and a plaid shirt opened the locked door. A badge was clipped to his waist along with a gun belt and pistol. He offered a hand to Devon, "Devon. There's nothing new to tell you at this point. We're following up some leads."

"We have information for you. May we adjourn to a more private locale?"

Surprised, he held the door open and waved us in. He led us to a small conference room and plopped down in a plastic chair and leaned back, looking expectantly at us.

"This is Shyenne de la Angelino, Alpha Female of the Salmon River Pride, member of the Nez Perce Coven and investigator with 3D Investigations in Lewiston, Idaho. This is Dylan Delrikkio, member of Nez Perce Coven and investigator with 3D Investigations. I called them in because two more women disappeared."

The feet of Detective Harrison's chair hit the floor. "When did you discover them missing?"

"Last night. I drove to Lewiston immediately and met with Shy this morning. They worked an investigation in Lewiston they believe relates to the disappearances," Devon explained, nodding towards me.

Detective Harrison directed his attention towards me, "You're a witch and a Were?"

Nodding, "Yes, I'm a fourth level Elemental witch and classified as a catalyst as well as a Were bobcat. 3D Investigations hired me due to my magical expertise. We worked with the Nez Perce County Sheriff's Department regarding magic users attempting to obtain illegal spell components, namely a Were pituitary gland. In the course of the investigation, we discovered an alarming trend of disappearing young adult Weres, mostly females. We uncovered who perpetrated the crimes and facilitated their arrests. Unfortunately, one of the witches escaped. He documented his..." I searched for the right word, "experimentations and the fantasies he harbored towards Were females. In a concealed laboratory in his basement, we found a woman locked in a cage. Devon's missing women match his preferred victim type: Were, female, young, thin, brown hair, attractive."

Detective Harrison stared at me for several moments, "Who did you work with at the Nez Perce County Sheriff's office?"

"Detective Swanson. I have his direct line and cell number if you need them," Dylan responded.

Glancing at Dylan, Harrison pulled out his cell, punched a few buttons, making a call. With my extra sensory kitty hearing, I heard a female voice answer, "Nez Perce County Sheriff's Department."

Harrison identified himself and asked for Swanson. After several moments, he came on the line. Glancing at Devon and me, Detective Harrison stood up and walked out of the room. A couple minutes later, the door opened and he returned. "Who accompanied you to Montana?"

"Currently, myself, Dylan, Tristan, Lance and Nate Kane," I responded. "Once we verify it is Scott Clark, we'll regroup with both covens and determine how to proceed."

"I've worked extensively with Dylan for the last few years

and Shyenne proved instrumental in solving the case relating to Scott Clark. I don't know if we would have solved it without her assistance," Detective Swanson stated. "Shyenne and her sister's involvement minimized injuries and deaths related to magical attacks. Their interpretations of the magical components of the crimes proved extremely beneficial to understanding the case. I recommend them highly and look forward to working with them again in cases relating to magic and Weres. Scott Clark is a very dangerous individual. He attacked us magically when we served the search warrant on his residence. Without Shyenne and Shaylenne, we would have been hit with a fireball. For your own officers' safety, witches need to accompany you any time you may be confronting him. To date, we charged him on six kidnappings and five murders. One victim he held captive in a cage in his basement for over a month. Our case is rock solid. We have a collaborator's confession, victim statement and his own written account of the activities as well as his father's and the other collaborator. Not to mention, numerous bottles of potion remnants with victim DNA recovered from his father's house."

Detective Harrison inhaled deeply. "Thank you for your information. We appreciate the heads up. We've experienced little involvement with Weres or witches. A case of this magnitude is definitely a first for us."

"Well, 3D Investigations provides the best personnel for back-up when it comes to this type of situation. They're very knowledgeable regarding magic, witches, covens and Weres. The people we came in contact with, held them in very high regard as well," the other detective advised.

"Okay. I'll let you know if we find your guy. Thanks, again." Harrison ended the call. "I'm not sure what you may find at the crime scenes. Our witch failed to glean any information."

"No offense to your witch, but she doesn't know what she's doing. We'd like her to accompany us and we'll teach her how to aid law enforcement in a situation involving magic," I responded.

Harrison looked at me, a little surprised and raised an eyebrow. He looked up a number in his phone and called it. I heard a female voice answer. "Where are you?"

She responded, "In the computer room."

"Come to conference room D. There's a couple witches I want you to meet." She readily agreed.

A few moments later, a stout young woman entered the room. She wore a uniform with her black hair pulled back tightly in a chignon. Eagerness shown through her bright blue eyes as she gazed at me and then Dylan.

"I am Celeste Mitchell, an earth witch level two. I don't belong to a coven," she introduced herself as required by coven standards.

Nodding, "I am Shyenne de la Angelino, earth primary, water secondary, level four and classified as a catalyst, member of the Nez Perce Coven and Alpha Female of the Salmon River Pride." She looked appropriately awed.

Dylan performed his introduction, "I'm Dylan Delrikkio, level undetermined, holistic magic, not yet classified, member of the Nez Perce Coven and investigator with 3D Investigations."

Unsure of herself, "I've never heard of classifications for witches before," she commented hesitantly, slipping into a seat at the conference table.

"I believe our coven is one of the few who uses a classification system. We employ its use to differentiate between the abilities each of us possess," I explained. "We're here at the request of Devon Ballantine in regards to the disappearances of four women from his pride. If you like, we offer to teach you better ways to utilize your skills aiding law enforcement with investigations."

Surprise and eagerness flitted across her face. "I would be honored to accompany you! I never received any formal education. I'm mostly self-taught and welcome any opportunity to engage with other witches!"

Harrison appeared surprised. "Alrighty then." Glancing down at his watch, "It's pretty late in the day. What say we start first thing in the morning?"

4

"**W**ant to start out in the Pralines and Cream room?" Devon asked me, in a deep, sexy growl.

I knew we would end up together by the end of the night. Studying him for a moment, "I'll leave it up to you. Seduce me."

A slow smile spread across his face. "Want to change into something… simpler?"

Meeting his gaze, I opened a portal to my closet and pulled out an emerald baby doll negligee. With a snap of my fingers, I changed from my jeans and sweater to the slip of lace. "Ready."

Devon's eyes melted a little as his eyes roamed up my bare legs to the silk skimming my thighs, barely covering my southern region. The negligee hugged my abdomen as it rose up over my breasts, with lace just barely covering my areolas. He stepped towards me, placed a hand at the back of my neck and pulled me in tight for a kiss. His lips gently caressed mine as his tongue forced its way into my mouth. His other hand encircled my waist, pulling me into him. My crotch met his large package. I moaned. Dueling tongues fought for dominance, his teeth scraped my lower lip, biting it. Abruptly he broke off our kiss.

"Come with me."

He took my hand and led me upstairs. We walked down a hallway, passing several doors and entered a darkened room. Unknowingly, I matched the color of my negligee perfectly to the room. Emerald green. Populated with men and women, most turned to see who entered. One woman was blindfolded, reclined on a chaise lounge, with a man eating her out while another one pinched her nipples as she sucked his cock. In a corner, a man stood in four point restraints while a woman blew him as a man fucked him. Another woman lay bent over an ottoman as a man pounded her ass while a woman sucked her clit and another suckled her tit. Instantly, wetness flowed between my legs.

A man and two women approached me. A petite red head blindfolded me as a Hispanic man led me towards a corner. Each arm was raised and placed into restraints. Lowered to my knees, my legs spread wide. And then, each leg, tied far apart. "No one fucks her but me. She sucks no man's cock." Devon ordered.

A soft hand caressed up from my knee, my thigh, under the skirt of my negligee. I wore nothing underneath. Tentatively, the hands brushed my inner thighs, while another set of hands tore the straps off my negligee, exposing my breasts. Two strong hands began to knead them, fingers massaging, pinching my nipples. I moaned. A gentle mouth covered one of my breasts, softly suckling, while the other one pinched the nipple, hard.

The hand at my crotch traced my folds, gently teasing my nub. As my juices flowed, she spread them from my clit to my anus. Each time her finger touched my ass, I whimpered. The man began to suck my tit, nipping and biting my nipple. A breast was thrust into my mouth. Eagerly, I pulled the nipple in, holding it with my teeth as my tongue flicked back and forth. The woman moaned.

The hands at my cunt became a little more forceful, rubbing harder, as one finger slid inside my vagina, then two fingers. I whimpered in frustration, but refused to let go of the nipple in my mouth. A finger slid up my ass. In surprise, I released the tit and ground my hips against the finger. Skin was placed against my mouth. I licked it. A female whimpered as I flicked her nub. I slipped my tongue down her slash and moved slowly, licking her, sucking her nub, just a patch of short curls tickled my upper lip.

"Spread your legs farther apart." I instructed her. She complied. I licked her from her ass to her clit, back and forth, several times. Her salty, sweet juice trickled down my mouth, neck and my breasts. The man sucking my nipples licked it up. The woman at my lower region suddenly sucked my nub into her mouth, scraping her teeth against it. I screamed in ecstasy as she forcibly suckled my clit. In return, I nibbled the button in my mouth, gently scraping my teeth across it as two fingers moved into my ass. The owner of the nub cried out as her orgasm overcame her. She fisted a handful of my hair, pushing my face into her pleasure box.

"Don't make her cum."

All ministrations stopped. I whimpered in consternation, sucking the clit in my mouth harder. She attempted to pull away but someone held her against me. I gently bit her clit, forcing her into another orgasm. Her juices poured into my mouth and down my throat as the other two licked them up. I felt someone move behind me. A hand wrapped around my throat, angling my head back. Devon kissed me harshly, squeezing my throat. The mouth transferred to my other nipple, biting it, then sucking the pain away as the mouth at my clit harshly nipped me. I jerked away, up against Devon. His mouth tightened at my throat, as he entered my cunt. The mouth ferociously sucked my clit as he pounded into me. When my orgasm hit me, his hand tightened at my throat, pushing me over the edge while a mouth held my nipple tightly between teeth. I bucked harshly against him, all of them, while wave after wave flowed over me. His hand loosened at my throat and I fell limp against the restraints. When I became aware, Devon held me by the throat and around the waist, pressed hard against his body with his cock still in me.

"Take me to your bed." I whispered, hoarsely.

5

The next morning, we travelled down a dirt road towards a small barn shaped house sitting within feet of the Bitterroot River. Tristan requested we park away from the structure. He began his hunt for clues in the dirt driveway. Lance, Dylan and I stood back from the house. Detective Harrison and Officer Mitchell parked behind Devon's Excursion. She walked up and joined us, eagerly.

"The first thing you want to do is determine if magic was used at all," Lance stated. "The best way to observe is by using your second sight. If someone cast a spell, you'll see remnants which will look like little bubbles in the area implementation occurred."

We all looked for signs of spells but didn't see any. "He didn't hit her with a sleep spell or anything from the porch," I concluded, turning back to the others.

"What about casting a detect magic spell?" Celeste inquired, gazing at me.

Lance and I shook our heads. "That just shows you anything magical or anything with a spell cast upon it within the vicinity but it won't indicate magic that already occurred," I explained. "Unless the caster disguised or hid a spell, second sight will allow you to see if there are any wards or traps." She made an "O" shape with her mouth. "Okay, we're ready to enter the house. Devon, did you lock it up?"

"Yes, I did." He moved to the stairs and unlocked the door, swinging it open to reveal a vase shattered and flowers strewn across the floor. An upended coffee table and large pieces of glass littered the couch, carpet and recliner. I smelled blood, two different types. Some appeared on the broken glass.

Dokwl perched on my shoulder. "Someone lost a battle in here," he commented, pointing out the obvious.

I agreed. "Okay, survey the room with your second sight," I recommended as I switched to mine.

"Wow! I see the bubbles!" Gleefully, Celeste responded, as she gazed about the small living room.

"Now, think about the most common spells you might see in a situation like this. Think about how the magic appears as you cast the spell. Search the bubbles for bits and pieces of magic you recognize." I coaxed the deputy.

Several moments later, she murmured, "A sleep spell?"

I nodded my head. "A good way to work on your identification of spell remnants is to cast spells in second sight. Then, you can observe the interactions between the components and magic. It'll help you in your casting, as well. Also, you'll notice where you make mistakes within the spell."

Celeste listened intently, nodding her head in understanding.

"The next part is extremely difficult. We want to attempt to identify the caster from the remains of the spell. Do you know how to recognize the sex and the magical orientation of the caster?" Lance asked her.

Shaking her head, Officer Mitchell responded, "No, I don't."

"Observe the bubbles closely. Notice the edges of the bubbles. How would you describe them?" I questioned.

Gazing at them in her second sight, she hesitated, "Rough, prickly."

"That's a male spell caster. Females tend to be softer and smooth." Lance remarked. "Now, to identify the orientation, look for elements, water, earth, fire and air. If nothing shows up, look for the most common types of magic you typically encounter. Shamanic, Wiccan, Voodoo, Druidic."

"I feel heat, fire." Celeste commented softly, as she studied the remnants of magic.

Lance and I nodded in agreement. I realized Dylan stood behind us, taking mental notes of the lessons. We recently unlocked Dylan and Malachi's magic. It had been bound since childhood. Theirs appeared very unique, untrained, wild, powerful. Uncle Al continued to observe them while determining their levels and classifications. Their magic seemed to be holistic, meaning they equally used all the elements. Both possessed significant inherent abilities, not limited to one or two elements. Uncle Al continued to research holistic magic as it appeared rarely. Ryan refused to answer questions regarding their mother. Malachi didn't remember her at all, Dylan's memories proved spotty.

"So, we have a male witch with fire as the primary element. Study the spell, memorize the rubs on the bubbles, the prickly parts, the way the bubbles float, hang suspended, remain, move." Lance described quietly. "These types of characteristics are used to recognize other spells cast by the same witch. These make up the profile, if you will, of the magic user."

Dokwl perked up, "This witch harbors ill intentions." One of Dokwl's inherent abilities, he comprehended the mage's intentions behind the spells.

I sighed heavily. "It's Scott Clark."

Lance nodded in agreement. "I concur."

"At this point, you learned all sorts of valuable information without casting any spells. Prior to casting, you want to ensure you gleaned as much knowledge as possible. Once you cast something, it convolutes the scene and becomes infinitely more difficult to pick apart who's responsible for what," I explained.

"What if the witch cast a clean-up spell?" Dylan asked, turning towards me.

"If the caster is higher level than you, you probably won't see anything. If he or she is lower level, then you'll see remnants of the clean-up."

Tristan entered the living room. Avoiding us, he performed a funny little dance, spinning, bobbing, punching, kicking. We all moved out of his way, retreating into the dining room. "Shy, c'mere. Answer the door. Lance, film me with your phone."

"If you want to learn to dance, Tristan, I can show you some moves!" Dokwl offered, performing several dance steps from my shoulder. I laughed.

Lance pulled out his phone. Raising an eyebrow, I walked to the doorway, he stood on the porch. With his right hand, he threw a pretend punch to my nose. "Toss your head back." I performed as instructed. As my head flew backwards, I saw blood at the top of the doorway and on the ceiling. I stepped back. Dokwl flipped off my shoulder, landing on Lance's. Trystan threw another fake punch to my nose. "You fall away onto the coffee table, breaking it. While you're down, kick me hard in the left kneecap with your right foot." I did a wild foot thrust to his knee. Tristan dropped down, crashing into the small end table beside the recliner, landing hard on his left elbow. "I hit you with a sleep spell. You're out!"

"Entertaining story. What makes you think all that?" Detective Harrison questioned sardonically from the doorway of the kitchen.

"But, wait! Our story isn't over yet!" Tristan remarked, gleefully. "Now, I pick you up and put you on my right shoulder." He bent down and laid me across his shoulder, then headed out the door. "After sustaining a serious injury to my knee, I experience difficulty navigating the stairs and drop you as I fall because I can't bear weight on the left leg well." He placed me gingerly on the ground, I allowed my head to loll to the left where I smelled blood. Were blood on the rock next to my nose.

"Here's a handprint where he caught himself with his left hand," he pointed at a hand print in the soft dirt, "and his hand gave out, causing him to land on his elbow, crumpling to the left." He indicated an area where it appeared someone had lain in the dirt. "He rises to his feet," pointing to tracks, "walks over to her, kicks her in the kidney, almost falls again, kneels down and maneuvers her over his shoulder and limps to the vehicle." He acted out the scene as he narrated. Once again, placing me over his shoulder. "At the vehicle, his left arm is injured to the point where he can't open the door. He plops her down, opens the door and then places her inside." Pantomiming shutting the car door, Tristan took a bow.

"We need pictures of all the marks in the dirt if we didn't mess them up," Detective Harrison stated, his voice awed. "Would you mind sending me that video?"

Tristan flashed a winning smile. "Would you like me to forward the pictures on to you, along with the correlating blood spots?"

Detective Harrison smirked, nodded and gave him the cell number. "Anything more we need from this site? Is it okay for me to send a crime scene unit out to gather blood samples, fingerprints, etcetera?"

I nodded. "We gained all the magic knowledge possible."

"Shall we head to the second abduction scene?" Detective Harrison inquired as his phone began pinging.

The final site where the last woman disappeared from was a secluded rustic log cabin set back in the pine trees. No neighbors lived within earshot or sight. The dirt road we drove up passed only a couple houses which lay back from the road, barely visible. "No one would have heard or seen anything that happened at this house," Tristan observed quietly, echoing my own thoughts.

Again, we parked away from the house. While Tristan surveyed the driveway, we walked along the edge of the road until we reached the clearing of her small yard. Detective Harrison and Officer Mitchell followed us. At the edge of the yard, we stopped to observe the house through our second sight.

"He didn't cast anything outside the house," Officer Mitchell observed. "How is he getting these women to let him in?"

Everyone was quiet for a moment as we pondered the question. "He is a good-looking guy. It looked like he performed a surprise attack on the last victim as she opened the door. Once inside, we'll be able to determine more." I responded, as I started towards the cabin.

Devon led the way to the front entrance, barely a stoop, no front porch. Unlocking the heavy wood door, he swung it open. No window or glass, not even a peep hole lay within the door. "She wouldn't know who she opened the door to," Detective Harrison stated, voicing my own my thoughts.

Inside, the house was trashed. Knickknacks scattered in pieces all over the living room. Broken furniture, a hole in the wall, shattered dishes, a bookcase tipped over, books thrown everywhere, pages ripped out, blood smeared the walls and the hardwood floor. My kitty olfactory senses identified two blood types, one the same as the last residence.

"What the hell? Why isn't he slapping them with a sleep spell as soon as they open the door?" Nate asked, stunned by the grisly scene.

"Because he wants the physical battle. That must be part of his M.O." Detective Harrison replied, eyeing the crime scene.

"He wants to create fear and cause pain to his intended victim. He enjoys the panic experienced by the woman," Dokwl explained, from his perch on my shoulder.

"He's still developing his M.O. We are seeing the progression of his developing signature. He realized he enjoys the physical battle," I added, almost overcome with nausea.

"Is he going to kill them?" Deputy Mitchell asked softly.

I shook my head. "Worse. He locks them in cages, repeatedly raping and torturing them. For months."

Detective Harrison turned towards me, "How do you know that?"

"I found one of his victims. She's a member of my pride now. He kept her for two months before we discovered her in his basement." The horrible stench of his evil laboratory haunted my nightmares. I still smelled the blood, fear, and excrement from all the Weres he tortured in the hidden little cell, behind the fake wall. I shuddered at the memory. I wanted to burn my nostrils to rid myself of the horrible odors etched into my brain.

"It was the worst site I've ever seen." Nodding towards me, Dylan continued, "Shyenne had to read through his detailed documentation of his 'experiments'. It was truly horrific."

"So, you think the women are still alive?" Detective Harrison questioned, as he leaned down, inspecting a pool of blood.

I nodded.

Gazing around the room, using our second sight revealed a number of spells. "It's a mess. Did he cast several spells?" Deputy Mitchell questioned, as she observed the magic workings.

"Yes. Search for the sleep spell first, since you know what that looks like," Lance suggested. "Once you identify the remnants of it, it's easier to pick apart what else he cast."

"Isn't he taking a big chance starting a physical altercation with a Were?" Detective Harrison asked Devon, evaluating the messy abduction scene.

"A very big chance. Hand to hand combat, I'd bet on a Were over a Witch every time," Devon stated, emphatically.

I nodded, agreeing, "He doesn't look like he works out or anything. He's about Lance's height and build. Lance possesses significantly more muscle mass than he does," I added. "Even a young female Were would best him, physically. But magic levels the playing field. In the end, he'll win, unless she has magical protection." Turning to Deputy Mitchell and Dylan, "Can you discern what other spells he cast?"

She shook her head, "I'm not familiar with a couple of them. Two seem similar. One is a levitation spell?"

"Yes," Lance responded, as he studied the mixture of spells.

The remnants of numerous spells floated around the room. The dissipating pieces hung in the air, slowly fading into oblivion. Discerning which parts belonged to what spell and identifying it required concentration and recognition. With four cast in the same area, the site was convoluted.

"Is it a healing spell?" Dylan asked. Surprised, Lance and I nodded. "Did he cast two of them? One stronger than the other?"

"Impressive. Yes. Shy, is the substantial amount of blood Were or witch?" Lance asked, indicating a large puddle on the floor.

"Witch." Devon and I identified together.

"So, he sustained a serious enough injury requiring he heal himself. He used the more potent spell on himself, and the lesser spell on her," Lance explained as we all observed the blood splattered throughout the room.

Tristan walked in the door, smiling. "Guess what he was stupid enough to do." He levitated a pine cone petal above his hand. "He left us his address."

"You can get an address from a piece of a pine cone?" Detective Harrison questioned with skepticism dripping from his words as Tristan swirled the pine cone petal above his hand.

"Great job, Tristan!" I turned to the detective. "More than likely. He cast a spell into the petal, using it as a charm. As an Earth Witch, I can identify the tree the petal came from. Using a locate spell, I can 'port through one pine tree to the tree that bore this. I know when I use petals, I walk outside my house or office and pick up a pine cone off the ground. I'm willing to bet, he did the same." Smiling, I observed the petal. I opened a portal to my office and picked up an evidence bag, dropping the petal in and zipped it closed.

"Wow. Things quickly went awry in here," Tristan noted, entering the house. "That's why he used the healing charm. Huh. And two healing spells." Tristan observed the room and began his inspection.

I showed Deputy Mitchell and Dylan the petal. "Using your second sight, do you see how the spell is the same as the first healing spell he cast in here?" The two studied the charm and nodded. "Now, identify the sex and magical orientation of the caster utilizing the spells and the charm."

"It's easier to figure out when there are more spells to study. And I recognize his casting signature! The same person cast these spells as the ones from the previous house." Deputy Mitchell determined, excited about making the connection.

Smiling, I nodded. "When you know what to look for and you're comparing to one you already studied, it's easy to recognize another spell cast by the same person."

"What about you and Shaylenne? Is it possible to tell the difference between the two of you?" Dylan asked.

"That's a great question. Actually, it is. Even though Shy and Shay are identical twins, Shy is an Earth Witch primary, Water Secondary whereas Shay is a Water primary, Earth Secondary," Lance explained.

Tristan stood on one leg in the middle of the broken knickknacks. "Technically, theirs look exactly alike except that Shy's have an earthy feel and Shay's have a watery feel. If you don't check for orientation, you wouldn't know the difference between the two."

"Good point. That's why it's always important to note orientation," Lance remarked, pointing to Tristan.

"Shyenne's magic possesses a chaotic feel to it while Shaylenne's holds a controlled, disciplined touch," Dowkl described further. Huh. I didn't realize that difference existed between us.

"That's interesting. With identical twins, the DNA is the same, so law enforcement couldn't use it to differentiate between them," Detective Harrison pointed out.

"We grew up learning magic together and automatically recognize each other's spells, without really thinking about the process. But for others, I can see where it could be an issue," Lance remarked. Returning his focus to the room, "Scott must have sustained a serious injury to use a spell in here and then a charm."

"He did, and here's why." Tristan leaned over the back of the couch, pointing to an object that fell behind it. "I'll let Mr. Detective handle this one."

Harrison rolled his eyes and looked behind the couch. "How about you levitate it up to me?"

"Okey, dokey. Always happy to help law enforcement!" Tristan brought the knife up. Harrison pulled a heavy-duty evidence bag from a pocket in his cargo pants and Tristan dropped the knife inside, carefully. "I think I worked out what transpired. Want to watch the show?"

We all nodded. Harrison pulled out his cellphone. "I'm videoing it. The last one proved quite informative."

Tristan walked to the door, I opened it. He play-punched me in the nose, twice. I stumbled back, knocking into the knickknack shelf. He advanced forward, "Grab a knife off top of the buffet with your right hand and swing it towards me."

Surprised, I followed his command, partially deflecting my blow, I hit him in the left side of his abdomen, barely. He punched me as he fell next to the pool of blood on the floor. I flew against the couch, hitting my head in the hole in the wall and the knife left a dent next to my head, dropping behind the couch.

"Sleep spell on you. I'm bleeding profusely. Do a major heal spell on me. I think you might have been rendered unconscious when your head bounced off the wall, but I performed the sleep spell automatically. I then cast a minor healing on you, targeting your head. I don't want to wake you, but I don't want you to suffer a severe hematoma and die before we have lots of fun. His point of view, not mine." Tristan clarified, glancing at me, wide eyed. "I'm still severely injured. The spell may not have worked, since I cast it directly upon myself. She appears to have stabbed him good. He grabs something to staunch the blood flow and heads to his vehicle." He squeezes his left elbow and arm against his side, catching himself on the door jamb, "Here, against the shrubby bush thing, blood," he pointed out as he stumbled and weaved out the door. "I'm hurrying to my car, taking long strides, note wide spread blood splatter within the grass. I parked over here, behind the garage." A large pool of blood lay next to a narrow set of tire tracks.

"Those tire tracks belong to a jeep," Nate remarked. "I drive a jeep. The tire tracks are narrower than most other vehicles."

"Wow. He lost a lot of blood! She must have cut him deeply!" Devon stated, as we noticed a significant pool of blood next to the tire tracks.

"Yep. I fumble with the door, finally pulling it open. I kept a healing charm in here and activate it. There's enough blood I don't have a problem initiating the spell," he commented wryly, as he pantomimes invoking the charm. "Once the healing finishes, I drop the charm here," he pointed to a spot in the dirt where a few minor drops of blood congealed. "I'm not going to die, but I'm weak, really weak. I must get out of here." Shooting an evil look over his shoulder, "But I'm taking her. I return to the house, leaving another spattering trail of congealed blood." He returned to the attack site

34

with us following. "There's no way I can carry her. I'm too weak. I levitate her out to the vehicle." He levitated me in the air.

"Really?" I rolled my eyes.

Ignoring my interruption of his monologue, "She doesn't leave much of a blood trail because I healed her broken nose. I levitate her out to the vehicle and she waits here in the air while I open the door and push the seat back for her, dripping some blood, there." He pointed to a few drops mixing with the dirt. Once again, he pantomimed slamming the car door and took his bow.

"So, is your classification the crime scene whisperer?" Detective Harrison asked, shutting off the video.

Wide eyed, Tristan turned to Lance and dropped to his knees. "Please, please, please, please, please! Can I pretty please with maraschino cherries and whipped cream in a white Russian, please, please have the classification of crime scene whisperer? Oh my gods! That would be totally awesome!"

Lance is second in command within our Coven, meaning he has input on classifications. He rolled his eyes. "He totally gets my vote," I threw in my support, trying to hide a smile.

"Fine, you can be classified as the crime scene whisperer," Lance stated, shaking his head. "But you get to inform your dad."

Tristan jumped to his feet, pumping his fist in the air, "Yes!"

"Did you happen to take pictures? The last ones you sent me were incredible. We need you to train officers how to photograph evidence at a crime scene," Detective Harrison commented.

Nodding enthusiastically, "I surely sure did! I'll forward them to you," ecstatically, Tristan scrolled through his phone, selecting pictures.

Tristan's heart is made of pure gold. His magical skills aren't on par with the rest of us. He tends to beat himself up over it. His father taught all of us our magic My mother and her father died during a coven ritual. Lance's father … he wasn't … right, injured in the same ritual. During the working, something went very wrong, with fatal consequences. Uncle Drew's mental capacity became impaired. A majority of the time, he proved incapable of performing magic. Sometimes, magic occurred, but not how he anticipated. Uncle Alberto stopped performing magic for years, until we displayed abilities. He really had no alternative. It was far too dangerous for us to experiment and learn on our own. And we couldn't be stopped. No matter how hard he tried.

At the time, Shay and I still held kitten form. We failed to transform into humans until adolescence. We were born as kittens instead of humans. In older Were generations, this was considered an aberration. An aberration to be euthanized. Or in our paternal grandfather's opinion, fed to our brothers. Luckily for us, Bane, our oldest brother protected us.

"What are you going to do now?" Detective Harrison asked as his phone began pinging, indicating Tristan's pictures arrived.

"We'll perform a locate spell on the charm, see what tree it leads us to," I informed him.

"Why don't you do a locate spell on Clark?" Deputy Mitchell asked.

"He conceals himself and will probably be alerted someone is searching for him. It's been tried numerous times since he escaped from jail but we aren't able to locate him," Nate spoke up. "Our coven did everything we could to try to find him. We realize the danger he poses to society while at large."

"I'm going to call a crime scene unit out here and touch base at the other residence regarding gathering evidence and DNA samples. Your Detective Swanson said he'd walk me through how to present a case with magical evidence to the county attorney and later, to the court. I really appreciate your assistance with this," Detective Harrison commented, surveying the crime scene.

"Sir, if it's alright, can I continue to follow them? I've learned more this morning than I ever learned growing up," Deputy Mitchell asked, waving a hand towards Lance and me.

He nodded. "It would be a tremendous benefit for us if you possessed these skills." He started towards his vehicle. "Don't go after this guy without notifying me first."

"We won't. Clark possesses a significant amount of power. Once we locate him, we'll need to formulate a plan between the two covens to ensure no lives are lost," Lance promised, rubbing the back of his neck. Lance detested magical battles. I knew he wasn't looking forward to the altercation.

"Just let my Clan take care of him," Snapping his teeth, Devon snarled.

I shook my head. "All he would need to do is drop a sleep charm in a hundred foot radius and your entire Clan would go night night. I realize it's hard to hear, but a Were doesn't stand a chance against a prepared witch. And I guarantee you, he's prepared. Shay and I, both Weres and Witches would be hard pressed to stand against him. When he broke out of jail, his father transferred all his magic to him. Now, he holds an exorbitant amount of power."

"Why isn't she here helping?" Devon asked, his face flushed with anger.

"From a male standpoint, what's hotter than gorgeous, identical twins? Add in a sociopath focusing on Weres and then factor in he could steal their magic. They are the trifecta of his darkest fantasy." Tristan flung his arms out, "What wouldn't he do to obtain the two of them? Fuck, we're lucky he hasn't zeroed in on them already."

"Let's return to the clan home and regroup. We can inform Uncle Al and Stephen of our findings and conclusions. They may offer advice before we do the locate spell on the petal," Lance redirected the conversation.

6

Initiating a conference call to the two coven leaders, Lance updated them on the progression of the investigation. "Do you all agree it's Scott Clark?" Stephen Kane questioned us. We looked around at each other, all nodding.

"Yes, Dad, we do. Through our own independent evaluation of the spell remnants, we all conclude the casting profile is identical to other spells we've independently witnessed him cast," Nate stated.

Sighing, "What's your next step?" Al questioned.

"Port from a pine tree through the earth and follow the locate spell to the tree the petal came from. Hopefully, it's in his yard," I succinctly informed them, shrugging my shoulders.

Several moments of silence met my plan. "He developed a comprehensive ward to protect his location. Our coven employed numerous locate and scrying spells, trying to find him after his escape from custody." Stephen pointed out.

"Yes, but we aren't searching for him. We're using an inherent ability to track a tree," Lance explained.

"Stay within the tree and the earth. Utilize the essence to mask your presence from his wards. If you materialize, you may set them off," advised Al. "Do not tip him off until we have a plan in place to confront him."

"What about staying in astral space?" Tristan suggested as he sipped a drink while we continued the conference call.

"He may have placed wards on the astral plane," Stephen said. "Why isn't he teleporting? By driving, he's placing himself at substantial risk of being seen or getting caught."

"When he escaped prison, he used a charm. Perhaps, he doesn't know how to teleport," Lance suggested.

"Without someone to physically demonstrate to him, he may not know how. We're still experiencing difficulty acquiring the skill," observed Nate.

"Any sign of Kiki or Rosie?" Al questioned, referring to the witches who aided Scott in his escape from jail.

Shaking our heads, "There hasn't been any sign, magical or physical, that anyone else accompanied him on the attacks," Tristan responded. "Did he ever work any magic involving astral space? Can he access the astral plane?"

Steve paused for several moments. "Not to my knowledge."

"In reading through his … journal regarding the kidnapping, torturing and killing of Weres he documented nothing indicating he utilized psionics or astral space." I noted, "His mother suggested to them they incorporate essence into the spell instead of harvesting Were organs. It didn't appear they even attempted to try."

"Hmm. That's interesting. Be very careful." As an afterthought, Al added, "Lance and Shy should be the only ones to go to alleviate the risk of tripping a ward."

"Actually, we need to take Tristan. He's proven incredibly helpful on the crime scenes, discovering significant evidence no one else realized," Lance replied. "Then, he pieced everything together, demonstrating how the abductions occurred. The Sherriff's office wants him to demonstrate how to take crime scene pictures."

"He's earned himself the classification as the crime scene whisperer," I added in a very serious tone.

Stephen laughed and I'm pretty sure Uncle Al rolled his eyes. He sighed over the phone. "Be careful and call us as soon as you return."

We decided Tristan should cast the locate spell, conserving Lance and

I's magic, just in case caca hit the air blower. We melded into a Ponderosa pine tree on the grounds of the clan home and sank into the earth. Following the spell, we travelled laterally, then vertically, following the mountains, crossing under the west fork of the Bitterroot River before ascending to the top of a mountain and arriving at said tree.

It's hard to describe the sensation of 'porting. Your essence, faculties and senses remain intact. Your physical self is reduced to atoms. Travel becomes possible when your atoms mingle with the earth and trees. You flow along. As far as I know, only witches with earth as a primary or secondary element can 'port in this manner. 'Porting through astral space and water are the only other options I'm aware of. With water as my secondary element, I can 'port through it as well. The skill appears very difficult to learn and master. Bane somehow stumbled upon the ability as a child. He taught the rest of us. For Shay and I, 'porting saved our lives on numerous occasions when our grandfather's anger endangered our existence.

Peering through the tree, we reached a large three-story cedar sided house encircled by a deep green lawn, ringed with tall Ponderosa pines. At some point, someone cut many trees down, clearing the area for the house. An expanse of windows overlooked a highway far below, with a row of hills and mountains facing it to the east, the rising sun. A red jeep sat parked under a carport attached to the house. A large deck surrounded the house. Three wide steps led to the main entrance.

This must be it, Lance 'pathed to us. *There's a ward identifying the perimeter of the lawn as a protected zone. It bars against magic users and Weres. It won't allow any in or out without a charm. But it doesn't extend under the earth.*

Looks like Scott cast the barrier, Tristan observed.

I'm going to peek into astral space, I responded, agreeing with their observations.

Don't! Lance stated but it was too late, as I drifted from the tree to the open essence of everything. No wards, no spells, no charms. I saw the outline of spells he cast within the yard, but nothing extended to astral space.

40

Astral space is clear. Let's go in and reconnoiter the interior of the house. I suggested to my cousins.

Shy, be careful. Tristan followed, hesitantly.

You two, stop. We must proceed cautiously. We can't alert him to our presence! We are not prepared to take him on at this time! Lance warned us, but followed behind. *Shyenne! You drive me fucking nuts!*

The interior of the house was beautiful. Hardwood floors stretched throughout with cedar paneling dividing the space into rooms. A beautiful kitchen with all new stainless steel appliances glittered as the focal point. A black granite counter top accented an island surrounded by character wood stools. The living room boasted a rock fireplace with a granite mantle reaching up to the second floor. A wide expanse of windows displayed the river winding its way along the highway at the foot of tall hills. Tristan moved to the windows, gazing at the view.

Tristan, check upstairs, Lance, this floor, I'm heading to the basement. Look for signs of the Weres, Rosie and Kiki. I ordered, dropping down to the basement.

Dammit, Shyenne, be careful! Lance 'pathed, frustration and fear colored his tones.

The basement appeared pitch black. I switched to kitty sight. Shelves filled with bottles lined the small room I entered. I shuddered. I hate small rooms. I found the wine cellar. Heading out the west wall, I hit dirt. Okay, so the basement wasn't the same size as the first floor. Returning to the cellar, I tried the north wall. A pool table occupied the main part of the room with a very large screen tv dominating the wall. What the hell is it with men and overly large televisions? Compensating for something? I smirked. Devon wasn't compensating for anything.

Focusing on the task at hand, I continued my perusal of the man cave. Recliners and bean bags scattered throughout the game room. Against the east wall of this room lay a bar with almost as much alcohol as a commercial establishment. A foosball table rested in a corner as did a piece of exercise equipment. A stair case led up to the main floor.

I tried sniffing the air, but picked up no scent of Weres. Returning to the wine cellar, I tried the south wall. It led to a laundry room, with a chute extending from the ceiling into a basket, catching the clothes. All reeked of Scott. No sign of female clothing. A washer and dryer stood against a wall and a table lay opposite them with piles of towels folded on top. Lance appeared next to me.

Scott's in his magic room on the northwest end of the house. I saw no one else on the main floor. I see you found his dirty laundry. Lance quipped.

I have one more direction to check. He followed me to the wine cellar. I went through the east wall. I recognized the smell instantly, from my nightmares. Were, fear, excrement, blood, semen. Just like his laboratory. My eyes adjusted quickly to the dark. Four cages built against the walls comprised of silver lined bars. I made out the outline of a woman in each. Two huddled together, holding one another through the bars, careful not to touch the silver. One lay on a thin mattress on the floor. I smelled dried blood, weakness, infection. The last one dug at the earthen floor with clawed paws. Pain scarred her face and she whimpered as she pulled dirt from the floor, creating a hole.

Immediately, I started to leave astral space to help them. Then, my world went black.

7

As quickly as I went out, I woke up, springing to my feet, throwing a punch at the nearest being. He deflected my blow. I dropped down, swinging my leg out to take out his legs. He jumped over mine. I rolled to the side, gained my feet and did a side kick. Again, he blocked my attack.

"Shyenne! Focus! It's me. Bane!"

I threw two more punches before his words sank in. Bane. My oldest brother. I stopped. Looking around, I realized I stood outside the clan home. In the back yard. How the fuck did I get here? The last thing I remembered were the women, in silver lined cages.

Whirling around I saw Lance. I moved towards him, but Bane grabbed me into a bear hug. "Let go of me! That fucker hit me with a sleep spell!"

"He had to. You were about to do something stupid," Bane stated, his arms, bands of steel, wrapped around me, holding me off the ground so I couldn't 'port. I seriously thought about kicking him, but realized I wouldn't do much damage.

"Let me go!" I screamed. "I have to get them out of there!"

"We will. But you can't go off half-cocked without a plan. I'll let you go when you're calm." Bane stated in the aggravatingly calm voice of his that said I was acting unreasonable and he wasn't letting me go until I became rational. Age old behavior pattern of ours.

Huffing angrily, I controlled my breathing. I knew he was right and Lance might have been correct to knock me out but that didn't mean I needed to be happy about it. Or admit it.

After almost a minute, "Alright. I won't kill him."

Bane let me go. Immediately, I dropped into the earth, popping up behind Lance, putting him into a headlock. He eeped as my arm tightened around his neck.

"Let go of him, Shyenne," Uncle Al and Stephen rose up from the earth.

I growled softly into Lance's ear, "Paybacks are a bitch, cousin." Roughly I pushed him away.

"He has the women locked in silver lined cages in his basement. One is seriously injured. We need to get them out!" I exclaimed, angrily, stalking towards the two coven leaders.

"I want to check out your observations and formulate a plan. You can't go after him unprepared. He will win. I guarantee you he already formulated a plan with spells in place," Al stated firmly.

"And back up contingency plans, as well. Was there any sign of Kiki and Rosie?" Stephen asked. Lance and Tristan shook their heads.

"I found the laundry room. All the clothes smelled of him. I didn't see any female clothing. I have no interest in those two idiots. We need to rescue the women he abducted. Not focus on Rosie and Kiki. They made their beds." I blurted out, angry and impatient.

"You will speak to Stephen with the respect due him. Kiki is one of his coven members who is unaccounted for. And we need to figure out where Rosie is." Al reprimanded me.

"If they're around, they'll substantially boost Scott's power base and pose a significant danger to us in any rescue we attempt. Their whereabouts must be factored into our plans," Stephen explained, pulling a cell out of his pocket. "Try another locate spell on Kiki." Ending the call, he turned his attention back to me. "I understand your feelings. We all want to free the women. But we know how dangerous Scott is. We must do this right."

"Let's go indoors and I'll perform a mind meld. I want to see what defenses he's set up. Lance, you're first," Uncle Al directed.

I huffed in impatience as we all filed into the great room.

Standing on either side of him, Al and Stephen entered Lance's open mind, studying his observations of the house. It took them several minutes. While they performed the meld, I went to the bar and poured myself a double shot of rum. They both opened their eyes and sighed heavily.

"He's sporting several new magic items. He's wearing a ring of protection against water and one against earth and a third against air. The talisman around his neck protects against Shaman magic. His bracelet boosts fire," Stephen informed us. "The bracelet and water ring I recognize as heirlooms from the Clark family. I know nothing about the others."

"He carries several charms: assorted healing and a few fireballs. The wards protecting the perimeter of his house are going to be fairly easy to get around. The vessel lies in the kitchen on the counter. You can 'port in through astral space and dispel it," Al added his interpretations of Lance's observations.

"You're next, Shy." Standing on either side of me, I granted them access to my memories of the reconnaissance mission. I felt the two enter my mind. Uncle Al had been there before and I recognized his presence. His presence felt paternal and protective. Steve appeared entirely different. His mind appeared inquisitive and honorable. I couldn't hear their thoughts, just felt their intentions. They observed as I surveyed the yard from within the pine tree and followed me through until we reached the room where I located the cages. They slowed my recollections, studying each cage and prisoner intently. Then, they focused me on the room, trying to ascertain how to physically access it, to no avail. Having gleaned all the intel possible, they gently exited my memories.

Back in the great room of the Bitterroot River Clan home, we returned to consciousness.

"Perhaps, if someone wouldn't have knocked me out, I might have located the entrance," I remarked, cattily. Cattiness came second nature to me. Literally.

"Nope, you would have transported into the cage with them. He spelled the dungeon. If you touch the bars or cast a spell without holding the charm, you automatically transport into the cell and he receives an alert that something entered," Stephen replied, shaking his head.

"In all actuality, Lance probably saved your life. My guess, he would steal your magic immediately, then teleport you and him away, using your abilities, and start all over with you as his prized possession," Uncle Al pointed at me, emphasizing his statement.

"Which is exactly why we try to beat it through your head to look before you leap," my other brother, Jaden threw in, helpfully. I flipped him off. Yeah, I'm an adult.

"What the hell are you two doing here anyway?" throwing my arms out to my sides, I demanded.

"Lance called us. His self-preservation instinct kicked in and he knew you'd come up swinging. He bribed Bane to wake you. I just came to watch," Jaden smirked, hands tucked in his front pockets, he rocked on his toes. Bane and I rolled our eyes. Jadan and I don't get along well. We take pleasure in each other's misery. Especially if we caused it.

"Getting in will be no problem. Freeing the women from the cages will take some doing. I'll start researching spells," Uncle Al declared, ignoring our typical verbal altercation.

"Wait, you need to check Tristan," I pointed to him.

Nodding in agreement, "Yeah, he's done really well on this investigation, finding stuff we all missed. Totally reenacted each abduction scene, perfectly." Nate remarked.

"He is classified as the crime scene whisperer," Devon added. Uncle Al shot him a sardonic look as Steve snickered.

Implementing the mind meld, the two coven leaders spent several minutes observing Scott's home through Tristan's eyes, then returned to the study.

Stephen looked down at the floor for several moments, attempting to control his emotions.

"Devon, come take a look at this," Al encouraged, inviting him into the meld.

Apprehensively, Devon walked over to Al. "How do we … do this?"

"It's similar to how we 'port, without leaving our own body. I'll lead you." Al's consciousness entered into astral space, then grasped Devon's guiding him into Tristan's memories.

"What's up?" Jaden inquired of Stephen.

He sighed. "Kiki and Rosie's spell books lay on the bedside table of Scott's bedroom. There was no sign of either of them in the other rooms upstairs or in Scott's."

That wasn't a good sign. Witches don't part with their spell books, voluntarily.

Devon exited the mind meld, laughing, "I know right where his house is located. He's off the East Fork of the Bitterroot River. I saw the Sula Peak Lookout."

"So, how are we going to free the women?" Tristan asked, reclining back in his chair. "We can get past the wards but I don't know how to open the damn cells."

We all pondered the question as we sat around the great room at the Bitterroot River Clan House. One of the female werewolves took drink orders and handed them out to everyone while we contemplated the issue.

"If Al and I design a dispel charm, together, it might work," Stephen suggested, optimism failing to accent his statement.

Shaking his head, "I don't know. If he entwined several spells producing the cages, one dispel may not work. We need time and plenty of components to experiment with." Al stated, frustration colored his tone.

"By 'porting in astrally, we can work on the bars. We can go in and out until we free them," Lance remarked.

"No, we can't. As soon as a spell is cast on the cages, he'll be alerted and the caster will be transported into the cells. I'm certain once inside, there's a magic dampening field. You won't be able to cast anything from inside. We must get it right on the first go-round. He'll take off once he's alerted to our presence." Al shot down the suggestion.

"Can we 'port through the floor, grab them and 'port back through the floor? It's earth," I raised an eyebrow.

Stephen shook his head. "The cages are spelled to keep anyone who enters, or tries to enter, in. The magic dampening field may preclude you from 'porting back out. 'Porting is a magical skill."

"What about melting the bars?" Nate offered.

Everyone pondered this. Then, Al shook his head. "It's a magical attack against the cell. You'd be transferred inside."

"I got it! We pull the iron out of the bars!" I suggested, jumping up. The members of the group looked at me like I lost my sanity. "What are the bars made of? Iron with silver mixed in. What's the earth made up of?" Opening the patio doors, I walked out to the lawn. As an earth witch, I can feel the individual components making it up. I separated them, bringing the iron to the surface, forming a pile.

Tristan walked away from the group, and followed my actions, with the same result. Flashing me a lopsided grin, he nodded. Jaden and Bane performed the same action, iron falling into a pile.

Nate hesitated. "I'm not an earth witch, but if you show me how you're doing it, I can probably learn." Tristan moved to his side and began explaining the process.

"Do you think that will work?" Excited, Lance asked Stephen and Uncle Alberto.

They looked at each other, pondering the question. "The spell bonds to the bars. By pulling the iron out, we're attacking the individual molecules, not the entire object. We aren't actively working against the spells," Stephen hypothesized.

"However, you're using an innate magical ability. I believe he will be alerted," Al remarked.

"We need a distraction." Nate offered up.

"Lance and I will attack him." Everyone turned to me. "We trip the wards. He comes to check it out. We keep him occupied…"

"While we rescue the damsels in distress!" Tristan finished off, jumping up and throwing a fist skyward.

"Uh, I don't like this plan," Shaking his head, Lance interjected, hands splayed out.

"What if I back the two of you up? Jadan, Bane, Tristan and Dylan can free the women," Nate proposed.

"What if we come up with a different plan?" Shaking his head, Lance offered as a counter-proposal.

"Shyenne is better at battle magic than any of us." Bane commented. "With Lance and Nate feeding her power, she can handle Clark at least long enough for us to 'port the ladies back to the clan home. If she takes him out, even better."

Lance groaned audibly. "I agree Shy responds faster in a battle scenario." Mentally, he weighed the magic of the three versus Scott. "Having Nate present might throw him off, his own coven standing against him."

"The pack can attack him physically," Devon declared. A chorus of growls from his clan supported his offer.

I shook my head.

"Honestly, dude, all we are is cannon fodder in this fight. As Weres, we will be in the way." Jadan stated.

"He'll knock us out with either a sleep spell or a fireball. Instantly." Bane added.

"Then, they'll have to try to protect the clan while distracting him, as we try to free the captives, and then try to 'port everyone back to the clan home," Dylan remarked, arguing against clan involvement.

Devon rolled his eyes. Tristan hit him with a sleep spell, dropping him to the ground. I smacked Tristan in the chest. Members of the clan jumped towards Tristan. I dropped a circle around him. Lance dispelled the sleep spell as Jadan and Bane took up a defensive stand between my circle and the clan.

"What the fuck?" Devon pushed himself up off the lawn.

"Exactly. I'm the weakest witch here. I spelled you that quick. You're only awake because Lance negated my magic. If he hadn't, you'd be asleep for a minimum of five minutes." Tristan paused for a moment, taking a deep breath, "Think what could happen to you, and your clan, if you're all incapacitated for five minutes during a magical fight. Fireballs, lightning, iceballs all flying around while you're all out cold."

I released my circle. Devon and a couple members of the clan moved towards Tristan. "Don't you dare come near my cousin. Of all my family members, he's at the top of my list for who I like. He coherently demonstrated what we were trying to get through to you. Do you understand that a Were stands no chance against a witch who can cast?"

"What about protection charms?" Disgustedly acknowledging the realization, Devon spit out.

"For what? Sleep spell, fireball, lightning bolt, delirium? We have no idea what he'll cast." Jadan remarked, throwing his arms wide. Then, in a more conciliatory tone, "Look. I know it's hard to take. I'm an alpha male, too. I won't tell you how many times Shy kicked my ass sparring when Bane let her use magic against me, but she won ONE HUNDRED PERCENT of the time."

"We wouldn't be able to do a general protection charm guaranteed to protect you against his magic. Since he received his father's magic, his power increased exponentially. Even with Alberto and I working together to make the charms, we couldn't create enough to completely protect three or four of you in the short time period allotted." Contemplating the situation, Steve stated, "It would prove most beneficial for us to create one charm. Give it to Lance and have Nate boost it as he sends his magic to him and he funnels it to Shyenne."

Devon turned away angrily and strode to the sliding glass doors. I watched him for a moment, understanding his feelings of being powerless to help his trapped clan members. "Why in the hell aren't you two going? You're the coven leaders!" Devon spat out, turning back to us.

The rest of us immediately chorused a round of "No"s .

"We can't risk them being compromised. If the worst happened, he could kill them, maim them, or worse, steal their magic. They are our last resort." I stated emphatically. Returning to our plan, "Okay, so you'll make us a protection charm. I have a large crystal we can use to focus the magic from Nate and Lance, channeling it to me. I'll grab it. He's a fire witch. We need to focus on water. Let's take a quick trip to the headwaters of the Selway River. It isn't far from here. We can fill our chis. The Selway is our river. We grew up on it. This will boost our power. Nate, Dylan, you do whatever you do to energize before a major casting."

"I thought you were an earth witch," Devon stated.

"Shy, Bane and Tristan are Earth primary, Water secondary. Shay, Lance and I are Water primary, Earth secondary," Jadan explained.

"I'll come with you guys. What works for you seems to work for Malachi and me." As an afterthought, Dylan suggested, "What about Shay?"

"No!" Bane, Jadan and I emphatically proclaimed.

Lance replied, "We'll have her come after the fact and help with clean up."

The next few hours we spent prepping by filling our chis, obtaining whatever magical accoutrements we felt necessary and dressing in appropriate apparel, i.e.: fireproof. Not surprisingly, I returned first to the clan home. In the yard, I pulled out the sword Bane and I had made. It wasn't exactly a sword. Kinda a cross between a Klingon Bat'Leth and a sword. Not as rounded, but just as many sharp pointy ends. Bane's hobbies included weaponsmithing. I liked to infuse magic into his creations. Shay and I had lived in a central American jungle for a while as kittens due to our grandfather wanting to kill us. We discovered a strange metal burrowed into the mountainside. Incredibly lightweight, but strong, Bane spent a long time perfecting the best way to mold the element into weapons utilizing water, pressure and diamonds. I enchanted mine with sharpness of ice, the pressure of the earth and the dexterity of water. Using a special cloth encrusted with diamond dust, I sharpened each of the points. The Weres watched me from a safe distance. Noticing me sitting on the picnic table, Devon walked out of the clan home and joined me on the patio.

"What the hell is that?"

"*Eadala*. Justice."

51

"Remind me to always do right by you."

I smiled.

8

The rest of the team waited in astral space while I entered the home. I popped out in the kitchen quick enough to grab the crystal empowering his wards and returned to astral space. Outside of the wards, I appeared. Using *Eadala*, I crushed the crystal and 'ported into his yard. Lance and Nate followed behind. Nate set a circle with a tether reaching from them to me, feeding me their magic through the crystal, amplifying the protection charm made by Al and Steve, offering as much protection as possible. Their energy empowered me, quickening my reflexes. The power rippled through me. I felt lighter on my feet as I sauntered towards Scott's porch.

Scott walked out his front door. Nonchalantly, he leaned against one of the wooden posts of the deck. "Well, well, well. If it isn't the Injun coven. I surmise you learned of my new... collection of Were dolls," humor filled his voice as he noted Lance and Nate's presence as well as mine.

I loathe being called Injun. And I discovered that I severely dislike the moniker Were dolls, even more. Stopping about ten feet from him, I pulled *Eadala*. "Scott Clark, you are under arrest for the kidnap, murder, rape and torture of numerous Weres. And escaping from jail. Drop to your knees, extend your arms straight out to your sides." I decided to try the nice way first.

He laughed. "You drop to your knees, bitch, and suck my cock. Took you long enough to track me down. How'd you find me?"

Okay, he wanted to talk. No problem. I love the part in the movie where the evil villain desires to spill his guts. "You need to police your pine cone

53

petal charms when you abduct women."

"You can track a pine cone petal?" He asked incredulously. He formed a fireball in his hand, but just tossed it from one hand to the other.

Just as nonchalantly, I spun *Eadala*, like a baton. I guess this is the part where we try to unnerve the other by displaying our skills. "It's actually an inherent ability for earth witches. Didn't you go to magic school?" I asked, bemused.

Scott rolled his eyes, still tossing his fireball. "With my father as a coven leader, the teachers didn't really care if I handed in my homework."

"Education is wasted on the undeserving," I observed. "We're not here to reminisce on your glory days. Are you going to surrender nicely?"

"Nope." He threw the fireball. The rest of our crew waiting in astral space headed towards the dungeon.

Using *Eadala*, I deflected the fireball, sending it flying into the pine trees as he threw several more in quick succession, all of which I negated. When he paused, I sent a barrage of ice daggers. He cast off most but a few hit my intended target. Advancing, I twirled *Eadala*, releasing a volley of snowballs and daggers. Scott fired back with balls of lava which I easily returned. Lava is earth. My realm. Ducking, the flaming balls dropped around him, on to the deck and hitting the house. He spouted off another round of softball size fireballs, as I continued advancing. As I hit most with *Eadala*, I decided to move in close, hand to hand range. I didn't think he could manage sword play. The downside was it would prove harder for me to deflect his spells, the closer I came. Some of the fireballs landed behind me. I heard a couple bounce off the shield protecting Lance and Nate.

Scott's attacks stuttered. He realized the rest of the team penetrated his dungeon. I swung my sword. He dodged, falling down onto the deck. Scott discharged a lightning bolt at me. I deflected most of it, but definitely felt a zing zip past me, hitting the circle protecting Nate and Lance. He sent a fireball over my head. Lance eeped as it bounced off the shield. I tried to shake off the damage from the lightning bolt.

Scott jumped to his feet, forming a flame as an extension of his hand, a flaming sword. I swung a wide arc with *Eadala*. He parried my swing, striking towards my legs. I jumped over the flame, sending my sword towards his head. He ducked and whipped around. His flaming sword contacted my thigh. I screeched as it burned through my pants. The stench of burning flesh assaulted my nostrils. With a backhand motion, I spun, hitting his left forearm, slicing it off at the forearm. Screaming, he let loose a volley of arrows alit with fire, dropping his flaming sword.

I deflected at least half, with two hitting me and I heard Lance cry out. Their barrier fell. Even though I was still pissed at him for knocking me out, he was family. I roared angrily, swinging *Eadala* back and forth. I clipped his abdomen, ducked and rolled against the railing of the porch, dodging his return of raining fire. But Lance and Nate received the entire blast. Both cried out in pain. The stench of burning clothes, hair and skin assaulted my nostrils. Sluggishly, I turned to face him.

We got the girls! We're returning to the clan home! Bane 'pathed to me. With one last back swing, I sliced into Scott's belly, then reached my feet, bounded over the porch railing, racing to Lance and Nate. Scott let loose a long, ear piercing scream. My team mates suffered severe burns. Lance appeared unconscious, definitely receiving the majority of the spell. Nate, unfortunately for him, still remained alert with burns covering his face, chest and one arm. I 'ported the three of us to the clan home.

We landed in the yard. I dropped *Eadala* as I quickly turned to them, assessing their injuries. Easily, Lance suffered more damage than Nate. Severe burns covered at least half of his body. I immediately started healing him. Bane rushed to us, surveying our injuries. Out of the corner of my eye, I saw all the women. The clan formed a circle, protecting them, half shifting into their animal form. Wolves, mountain lions, bobcats, coyotes and lynx jumped in front of the circle, promoting the first line of defense for the clan. Devon transformed into a mountain lion, jumping to the forefront of his pride.

Before I could voice a warning, I felt Scott appear. He quickly looked around, noticing the Bitterroot River Were Clan and most of the Nez Perce

Coven. Blood and goo poured from his stomach. Then he disappeared. I jumped into astral space, chasing him. Just as I caught up to him, he disappeared. He dropped out of the astral plane into some sort of protected shelter. I popped out and surveyed my surroundings. The Clark family home.

I ran up to the front door and pounded on it. Mary opened it after a few moments.

"Shyenne! What are you doing here?" She asked, surprised.

"Where is he?"

"Where's who?"

"Scott! I followed him here through astral space! He went into some protected spot. Where is he?" I screamed at her.

"I... I... I don't know! I don't know where he could be!" Mary replied, flustered, shocked and stammering. Stephen appeared next to me.

"You deal with her. Kayla!" I cried out, heading up the winding staircase to her room. She ran out and met me. "Scott 'ported into a protected area somewhere near here. Where would he be? I couldn't follow him in!"

Hesitating a moment, "The safe! Follow me!" She ran down the stairs. Her mother grabbed her arm.

"No!"

"Mary! Stop. He is wanted by the police in connection with the kidnapping, rape and murder of five Weres. He escaped from jail. We just freed four more Were women he held captive. If you interfere you are jeopardizing your own standing within the coven, not to mention interfering in a criminal investigation." Stephen informed her, as the leader of the coven she still held membership in.

Burying her head in her hands, she began crying, stepping aside.

"Kayla, where did he go?" I asked his sister, grabbing her arm.

She raced through the kitchen and out the back, with me close on her heels. She led me to a beat-up old cellar. Performing some intricate hand signal, she opened the door. He 'ported out as we entered. I jumped into astral space but he was gone. No sign of him. Sighing in frustration, I returned to the cellar.

"Right off, I know he took several major healing potions, an energy regeneration ring, and a talisman of healing." Kayla informed me. Looking around the room, I saw a pool of blood and goo, from the evisceration I supplied him with. She inhaled sharply at the sight, then turned her eyes to me, silently asking for an explanation.

"For you and your mom's sake, I apologize. I," I hesitated, "distracted him while the women were rescued. Lance and Nate suffered severe injuries from his attacks."

"You did as well. Take me back with you. I'll help where I can. With healing, energy boosts, locating him. Whatever," she stated, resignedly. She ran a shaky hand through her hair.

We needed her help, but I hated pitting family members against each other. "Kayla, you don't have to."

"Yes, I do. A lot of these people he hurt because of me. I need to do what I can to fix that." Kayla replied, steel conviction lined her words as she straightened her back.

I sighed deeply, "He hurts people because he's a psychopath. It has nothing to do with you."

We returned to the clan home. As we landed we saw Scott standing next to Tristan. Blood and other bodily fluids poured from his abdomen. His left arm was missing the lower half. He threw a fireball and grabbed Tristan with his right arm. And disappeared.

"No!" Jadan, Al and I chased after him. But they left no trace.

We spent hours trying to find their trail to no avail. Finally, Jadan forcibly made Al and I return to the clan home. Completely drained, I sank to the ground. My injuries healed somewhat from my Were genes. Jadan grasped my right hand and transferred almost all of his energy to me.

"Thank you." I jumped up to return to astral space.

But he stopped me. "Shay! You and Shy search for Tristan. Don't blindly search. Go into astral space and call for him!"

Nodding, I glanced around, surveying everyone's magical force. Bane continued to deal with healing Lance and the two injured Were women. Stephen had returned from speaking with Mary and focused on healing Nate. Dylan's energy level remained full. Al used hardly any of his magic while Kayla remained completely full.

"Kayla, Dylan, Al! Come with us!" The five of us entered astral space. "Al, you're the lead. Dylan, Kayla and I will send our energy to Shay. Shay, boost Al. Everyone feel for Tristan," I directed. Using all of our energy we reached for him. But found nothing.

After several minutes, Jadan tried to reason with us. "Guys. We aren't going to find him this way. We need to conserve power. Let's return to the clan home and regroup." Shay nodded in agreement.

"No! We can't leave him! We can't!" I screamed, near hysterics. Al grabbed my hand and pulled me after him. I gave into him as we zoomed through astral space faster than I ever travelled before. Whether due to my injuries or lack of energy, at some point I passed out.

When consciousness returned, I felt something wrapped tight around me. Encompassed by safety, comfort, security. Reaching a hand up, I pulled his head down to me, melding my lips into his. He transferred energy into me. Someone had healed my burns while unconscious. His energy seeped into my soul. Malachi. I breathed in relief. Slowly, I opened my eyes, drowning in his mossy covered pine tree eyes. He sat cross-legged on the ground with me in his lap. Bane, Jadan and Dylan stood guard over us. I wrapped my arms around his neck, burying my head into his shoulder. I spent almost a minute drinking in his aura before I jumped to my feet. "Tristan!"

Malachi stood before me, enveloping my vision, focusing me. "Stop." He stated softly, but firmly. I halted, looking up into his eyes. "We're regrouping. We're coming up with a plan. We are not flying off willy nilly into the great unknown."

Twirling around, I saw Uncle Al sitting on a chair, holding his head, drained. Shay and Bane appeared pretty well completely drained. Jadan and Dylan had some energy left, but not much. "You're all too low. You already did the whole instinctual thing. Now we need to approach this from a logical standpoint. We've talked to Kayla. As his sister, she has ideas where he may have retreated to."

9

Tristan shook the grogginess from his head, sitting up. He felt completely empty. No magical energy. *That bastard drained me.* Looking around, he realized he was in a small cottage. He didn't recognize his surroundings. "What in the hell?" Confused, he searched his memory, trying to make sense of what happened.

The four of them entered the dungeon. Simultaneously, they pulled the iron out of the bars of the cages. It took several minutes before the iron separated from the other minerals. Once the cage front disappeared, they each 'ported a woman back to the clan home. Then the situation turned chaotic. The Were Clan surrounded the women. Bane jumped in to heal the most injured person, Lance. Tristan ran towards Nate. Shy screamed as Scott appeared. He disappeared with Shy chasing after him. Tristan focused on performing a healing spell on Nate. Second and third degree burns covered a good part of his body. After the first spell, Tristan gathered more energy from the earth to perform a second. Scott reappeared and grabbed him. They hurled uncontrolled through astral space. He remembered struggling, trying to get away from him before Scott slapped him with a sleep spell.

Surveying the room, Tristan sat slumped in a green easy chair. Scott lay passed out on a couch, blood and goo pooled around him and on the floor. Tristan swallowed the vomit rising in his throat. Quietly, Tristan rose to his feet and crept to the entry. Looking out the window, he saw trees surrounded the area. He opened the door, stepping onto the porch and down into the yard. Immediately, he sucked up as much energy as possible, filling his earth chi and tried to sink into the ground. But he couldn't. He entered astral space and tried to pass through the barrier, but hit a magical brick wall. He walked over to one of the large pine trees, slipped into it and tried to port. No luck.

Damn. He has it warded. Better than his house in the Bitterroot. Tristan walked the circumference of the barrier. A very tight diameter surrounded the house. Maybe fifty feet. He tried calling out for Shy, for his dad. Nothing. The forest smelled … minty, almost like mentholated. Witch Hazel enveloped the branches and trunks of various types of tall standing pine trees. Studying them closer, the undergrowth, the temperature, the humidity, Tristan surmised Scott teleported them to Oregon or southern Washington, along the coast. His family was in Idaho and Montana. A little too far away to 'path without a boost. In one of the pine trees, he noticed a beehive.

Fuck. Nowhere to hide. Nowhere to go. Dejectedly, he returned to the cabin. He searched for a crystal. It could work to boost a telepathic communication to his dad. To no avail. The only magical items, Scott wore. Surveying his captor, Tristan realized he was alive, barely. Obviously, he lost a lot of blood. And other unrecognizable bodily fluids. One of the rings he wore, should have worked to heal his injuries. But he hadn't activated it. The lower part of his left arm had become detached, with the stub burnt. A deep gash split his abdomen apart. He recognized the work of Eadala. *Good job, Shy!*

Tristan asked himself, *What do I do next? Search the house. See what I can find. What are my options? How the fuck do I get outta here?*

It didn't take long for Tristan to exhaust a search of the cottage. The house comprised of one bedroom, a bathroom and an open kitchen leading to a living room. He turned on the faucet and water flowed. Pouring himself a glass, he drank it down. And three more. It was well water, no chemical additives or filtering, just pure, natural water. That was good and bad. With his earth chi and water chi both full, his confidence rose. He didn't find the item fueling the ward around the cabin. Or a phone.

Hunger gnawed at his belly. Opening the fridge, he found mustard, pickles and horseradish.

This is worse than my fridge. He thought, rolling his eyes. *At least I have beer.* His search of the cupboards proved a little more fruitful. A package half full of pancake mix, a couple cans of assorted food, coffee, cocoa and tea. Honey outside in the tree. *Pancakes, it is.*

About twenty minutes later, he heard groans originate from the couch. Aside from cooking pancakes, Tristan spent the time convincing himself he could handle this. He needed to be friendly, joking, himself. If he was too likable, maybe, maybe Scott wouldn't … Himself. The personality that kept Shy laughing and grounded. He took a deep breath, nonchalantly, "Yo, dude, coffee, cocoa or tea? Pancakes will be ready in a few."

Out of the corner of his eye, he saw Scott struggle to sit up, then flop back against the couch, moaning. Tristan prepared him a cup of tea, adding some honey and headed to the couch.

"You're a fire mage, right? Here, warm your tea," Tristan held the cup out to him.

He hesitated, then took it. With tremendous effort, he heated the mug. Inwardly, Tristan smiled. Scott suffered severe injuries and retained little energy. This bode well for Tristan. He returned to the kitchen and flipped the pancake. "Dinner will be ready momentarily. Your kitchen didn't offer too many choices so we're having a gourmet meal of Flapjacks with mountain honey and a side of fried spam, guaranteed to make everyone thankful for IHOP!"

A painful chuckle burst forth from Scott followed by a whimper. Harsh ragged breaths emanated from the couch while Tristan made a plate for him. Pasting an easy smile on his face, Tristan handed him his dinner. Scott made a strange noise and Tristan turned back to him. "What the fuck is that?"

Tristan glanced at the plate. "Oh, our Granny Irene, well she really isn't our Granny. She's our housekeeper, but we've had her since we were kids. She says its poor presentation to serve a dinner plate without a garnish. Our choices for garnishments are severely limited. You have a pickle with a mustard smiley face and pine needle mohawk. I recommend strongly not eating it. Purely for aesthetic purposes."

Scott chortled, then whimpered. "Stop making me laugh. It hurts too much."

Weighing his options, Tristan decided to gain some good will points. "I'm not the best, but I do know a few healing spells. If you like, I can cast some to help you."

Scott considered his offer. "I have no way to escape. Your ward has me trapped. Or obviously, I wouldn't be doing a stint as a short order cook. Harming you is not in my best interests as I'm stuck here with very little options for food. While I'm sure my family is actively searching for me, I don't know when they will arrive. So, we might as well make the best of our time together. I hate to see anyone in pain."

Scott continued to hesitate. "Suit yourself." Tristan placed two pancakes on his plate with fried spam and poured honey over it all. Plopping down in the old olive green Lazy Boy, he dug into the food with much gusto.

Scott stared at him, eyebrows raised.

"What? I'm starving! Even if it's pancakes and spam. This is as gourmet as we're going to get." Tristan forked a bite of spam into his mouth and chewed. "Unless you're making a Taco Bell run?"

Scott continued to stare at him.

"No? Damn. Well, bon appetite."

We set up watches at the portals where Tristan might pop up. Zeke, Nate's youngest brother and their mother, Sarah went to Al's house to wait by the altar in the garden, in case Tristan showed up there and needed assistance. Sarah suffered a severe injury during a coven circle spell, permanently affecting her impulse control. Someone from her family or coven stayed with her at all times. While only thirteen years old, Zeke displayed a lot of promise as a witch. He proved very adept at aiding his mother in controlling her magic.

Rhiannon and Eraina kept watch over the portal at our lodge. Eraina was a teenage runaway befriended by a sorcerer trying to resurrect an Aztec god. We became involved when the sorcerer kidnapped a distant relative of ours. Once the sorcerer had been thwarted, I offered Eraina a safe home and magical education. She accepted. Rhiannon was the werewolf we rescued from Scott's evil laboratory.

With Kayla's assistance, we spent the next two days 'porting to every vacation spot, family member or place Scott expressed an interest in seeing. But we found no hint of Tristan. Shay and Lance worked on a boosted locate spell with Al and Stephen adding more oomph to it, hopefully, to penetrate whatever shields Scott hid behind. Nothing. Dylan and Detective Harrison combed through Scott's rental house, searching for any clue pointing to another location. Nada.

10

The next morning, Malachi returned to his tour. From the great room of the Bitterroot River Clan Home, I called Marcus Denton, Pacific Northwest Regional Alpha, on the big screen via vid phone. In short, he's the big cheese for all the Weres in his area. He makes and enforces rules, coordinates between all the packs, clans, prides, herds and flocks and is the public face of Weres to the rest of society.

"Shyenne de la Angelino. Why are you calling me from the Bitterroot River Clan home?" Straight to the point, the middle-aged wolf appeared on screen wearing a suit and tie. I felt the urge to choke him with his own red and grey striped noose.

"Funny that." I snorted. "Do you recall about four months ago, I contacted you regarding a witch name Scott Clark? Psychotic, kidnapper, rapist, murderer that escaped from jail?"

He rolled his eyes and didn't answer. Oh my god. He rolled his eyes at me!????

"I'm in Montana assisting with locating and retrieving four women who went missing. The women are members of the Bitterroot River Clan. Devon Ballantine, heir apparent, never received the warning I passed onto you." I paused. Marcus still said nothing. "We found the women. Clark kept them in silver lined cages. He repeatedly raped and tortured them. One suffered serious injuries."

"A witch is no match for a Were. If these women can't defend themselves against a witch, they have no business being a Were. Survival of the fittest." He responded flippantly, swirling a finger in the air. Such a regal move for an ass hat.

"Really." I replied, deadpan.

I think I heard Lance mutter, "Oh, shit," before I jumped to astral space and reappeared in the clan home in Seattle, behind Marcus.

"Fuck." That was Jaden. I saw my brothers and Devon on the screen back in the Bitterroot while I stood in Seattle. They watched the screen, open-mouthed, horror struck.

I placed Marcus in a choke hold and 'ported back to the Bitterroot. On the vid screen, his men ran around like chickens with their heads cut off, trying to determine what happened to him. I let go of him as he attempted to elbow me in the stomach. I swept his legs out from under him and he fell to the ground. Our eyes locked. Go big or go home. I hit him with a sleep spell, rendering him unconscious. Wide eyed, frozen, Bane, Jadan and Devon watched. Denton's men yelled over the screen, threatening me if anything happened to the big cheese. Ordering me to return him immediately. Silly rabbits. I don't take orders or give into threats. From anyone.

"Damn it, Shyenne." Lance muttered, shaking his head, wide eyed, hands splayed at his sides. "What the fuck?"

"I'm taking this opportunity to provide him with a valuable life lesson," I explained. The three male alphas, Devon, Jaden and Bane stood silent, frozen, unsure how to proceed.

Shaking his head, Lance walked to the forefront of the screen. "Gentlemen, we assure you no harm will come to your big, bad boss man. Shyenne merely demonstrated that a witch can easily overpower a Were." Lance turned to me, "Shy, how long is he going to be out for?"

"Only a few hours." I answered sweetly, smiling to the near apoplectic Weres in Seattle.

Lance stared at me, horror struck. "Let's not start an interspecies incident," he whispered under his breath, leaning down next to the unconscious man. Grabbing him by his tie, Lance returned Marcus to the Seattle home.

The Weres rushed him. As an act of self-preservation, Lance dropped them all with a sleep spell.

Expletives, moans and groans chorused from the alpha peanut gallery. I laughed uncontrollably. Lance shot a sheepish look to us over the vid screen. He stood up, scratching his head.

"Oh my god. This is a fucking train wreck, but I can't look away," Devon commented quietly, staring at the screen. "I honestly don't know what to do."

"If this wasn't our little sister and cousin, I'd laugh my ass off," Jadan rubbed his face, shaking his head. "Where's the popcorn?"

Bane whispered, "Fuck. I guess it's time."

"Time for what?" Jadan asked, glancing at his brother. Bane didn't respond.

Lance hesitated for a number of moments, formulating a plan. He dispelled my sleep spell on Marcus and quickly 'ported back to us. Marcus jumped to his feet, spinning around. His four men, fast asleep on the floor.

"What the fuck do you think you're playing at, little girl?" Flustered, Marcus whirled back to the screen.

In a calm, quiet voice, I replied, "I am demonstrating that a witch can easily take out a Were."

"Or four. I, too, received an education of witch vs. Were in a combat setting. As was pointed out to me, even the weakest witch," Devon stated harshly, "can easily take out an alpha Were."

I swear, I could almost see steam billowing out of Marcus' head. "And now, Clark is in the wind. He kidnapped my cousin. He's going to be looking for more women. Do your fucking job and warn the clans about him." I yelled, then hung up on him.

"Oh my gods. She just told off the regional alpha." Bane observed quietly, completely awestruck.

"Fuck. Some days it really sucks being your older brother," Jadan observed, grimacing.

I rolled my eyes.

11

Scott fell asleep on the couch shortly after finishing dinner. Staring at him, Tristan considered his options. If he killed him, the ward might drop. 'Course, it might not. The food situation was rather dire. Three to four days left, at the most. If Tristan could observe him taking down the ward or figure out where it originated, he could escape. The healing process seemed rather slow. Scott must not be able to heal himself directly. That made sense. At the crime scene he dropped two healing spells. He ended up using a charm as the spells didn't work to heal himself. For some reason, it was fairly common that witches couldn't directly heal themselves. His magical energy was slowly returning, slower than Tristan expected. Probably due to his injuries.

Focus. What would Shy do? Tristan contemplated the situation. *She would find the ward, figure out the energy source and how best to disarm it.* So far, Tristan knew the ward surrounded the cabin in a tight circumference. Returning to the Wards 101 class of his youth, for a ward like this, effecting a specific area in a circular field, it usually fell at the epicenter of the area.

Gazing out the window, he judged about an hour of good daylight left in the day. Jumping up, he returned to the kitchen and rummaged through a junk drawer, locating a tape measure. He glanced at Scott as he quietly exited the cabin. Starting at each corner of the house, he measured the diameter from the edge of the barrier to each corner. Equidistance of thirty feet. He returned to the cabin and carefully measured the interior corners diagonally and found the center. A cupboard in the kitchen. The cupboard contained plates, bowls, cups and glasses. Detecting magic on the area revealed nothing.

Perhaps, I'm not strong enough to detect his magic. If he cloaked the ward, I wouldn't see it. Scratching his head, he contemplated the situation. *If I touched a magic item, it may zing me. Or I might feel the energy coursing through it.* He surveyed the cabinet filled with dishes. Rolling his eyes, he individually picked up each item, studying them for any sign of magic.

"What are you doing?" Scott inquired groggily from the couch. He attempted to straighten up, whimpering in the process. He flopped back down.

"Uh, I thought I heard a mouse scratching around in here. I'm seriously freaked out about Hanta Virus, so I'm checking all the cupboards for mouse droppings. I'm OCD like that," Tristan hastily improvised. "How ya feeling?"

"Like your fucking cousin eviscerated me and cut off my fucking arm," Scott proclaimed, with a labored breath.

Nodding his head, "Karma's a bitch. Want that healing spell yet?"

Scott shook his head. "I need to piss."

"Want a hand?" Tristan started laughing, "Sorry dude, no pun intended." Tristan walked over to the couch and assisted Scott with reaching his feet. "I'll help you to the bathroom but I'm not holding the family jewels. You'll have to figure that out on your own."

Scott grunted in acknowledgement. Tristan closed the door behind him and quickly continued his search for the ward. Several moments later, the toilet flushed and the door opened. His pants remained undone. Blood and goo covered them and his shirt.

"You need to clean up. You'll get an infection. Especially with that mix of bodily fluids near your open wound," Tristan observed. "Cast a clean up spell on yourself."

"I drank several healing potions. Won't that take care of it all?"

"Uh, no. The potions boost your own white blood cells and metabolism to speed up the process. But that shit near an open wound will start an infection, creating an entirely different "wound" than you originally began treating. You need to clean up the injured area, keep sterile bandages over it, treating it as you would normally, along with potions, charms and spells." Tristan explained. After a moment, "Didn't you graduate from Magic School? Don't you know this stuff?"

Scott sank back onto the couch, whimpering at the movement. "Studying wasn't my forte. I passed because my father was the Coven Leader."

"What about all the healing spells you performed for Kayla?" Tristan questioned, surprised he retained so little actual basic magical knowledge.

He shook his head. "She didn't have wounds. We attempted to treat her diabetes. I focused mainly on," he hesitated, "procuring necessary spell components."

"Kidnapping and torturing Weres." Tristan stated dryly, with a slight sneer. He leaned back against the kitchen counter, thinking Scott was the epitome of a psychopath.

"Potato, potaaato, tomato, tomaaato," Scott commented. His voice sounded almost bland, except pain crept in.

Swallowing his disgust, Tristan asked, "So, are you going to cast a clean-up spell on yourself?"

Scott mumbled something and waved his hand. Part of the gore disappeared.

"Is that all you got?" Surprise colored his statement. Tristan performed the minor spell, removing the rest of the bodily fluids. With another spell, he removed his clothes. Grabbing a blanket from the bedroom, he threw it over Scott.

"Why are you helping me?"

"Because I'm trapped in this cabin. We have food for maybe four days. I don't know if you die the ward will drop. I don't want to die out here, with you," Tristan stated bluntly.

"Transfer some of your power to me."

Tristan laughed. "Uh, no. Not voluntarily, asshole. If you want, I'll cast a healing spell on you."

Scott hesitated, then nodded. "Thanks."

Tristan executed the spell. Scott's body visibly relaxed. "I'll see what I can find for bandages. What the hell did you do to your arm?" Tristan noticed the stub appeared burned.

"I cauterized it. I know I should have cauterized my stomach too, but I just couldn't."

Tristan shuddered as he entered the bathroom. He found a bunch of gauze and hydrogen peroxide in one of the cabinets in a first aid kit. After washing his hands thoroughly, he poured the peroxide over them and returned to the living room.

"I'll pour the hydrogen peroxide on the gauze and place it on your wound." Scott nodded, grimacing as he watched Tristan's actions. Gnashing his teeth together, he tried not to scream as the gauze settled over his abdomen. Once Tristan finished, he covered the stub of his arm.

Between his teeth, "Hit me with a sleep spell," Scott whispered through the pain, "Please."

Tristan acquiesced. Returning to the kitchen, he continued his search for the ward. After about twenty minutes he heard voices coming from the living room. The television turned on. *That's weird.* It appeared to be on a kid's channel, some obnoxious game show. The remote lay on the arm of the chair where he had eaten dinner earlier. He clicked through the channels until he located music, then returned to the kitchen. As he entered the kitchen, the television returned to the previous channel. *What in the hell?*

He flipped the channel back. Feeling a force on the remote, the game show began blaring again. Dropping the remote, Tristan quickly glanced around the room, but saw nothing. Confusion colored his features momentarily before he slapped himself in the forehead. "I didn't follow my own advice." Switching on his second sight, he saw a scrawny purple creature with a long tail and four legs. Covered in scales, light shimmered almost iridescently over the diminutive body.

Tristan squeaked and vaulted over the couch, crouching behind it. "What the hell are you?"

The thing "eep'ed" and with gossamer wings, flew, landing beside Tristan, cowering behind the couch, too. Tristan backed away from it. Their eyes locked.

"Wait! Can you see me? You can see me! Yah!!!" It flew to Tristan and wrapped its front legs around his neck, hugging him. His scales felt leathery against Tristan's skin. The thing hastily let loose of Tristan, flying backwards. In a lower tone of voice, "That's cool, Dude. It gets real boring around here." Jerking a clawed digit towards Scott, "That scummy ball sack is a freak! I stay away from him."

In shock, Tristan stared blankly at the creature. "You do see me, right?" Tristan nodded. "You do speak. I've heard you." He hovered at eye level, studying Tristan. His iridescent gossamer wings appeared fragile. Tristan wondered how the delicate appendages could carry the tiny dragon.

"What… who… how?" Stuttering, Tristan cautiously relaxed a little. He stared at the creature, lizard, tiny dragon? He didn't recognize what type of animal appeared before his face, flying on impossible wings. He reached a finger out and poked him in the belly. It giggled.

"A real rocket scientist, huh? You can call me J-Dawg, like the letter. My actual name is long and difficult for humans to pronounce." Puffing up his chest, as big as a two-foot creature can, he announced, "The English translation for my kind is a light dragon."

Confused, Tristan clarified, "As in a small dragon?"

Scoffing, "No, as in the sun, light bulbs, etcetera." J-Dawg's body began to glow, illuminating softly. His scales looked like mother of pearl, with a purple hue. His front appendages had two digits and a thumb, for grasping. Razor sharp nails tipped the ends. His hind legs sported three toes and a thumb, for perching, with sharpened claws. His nails emanated a plum tint. Down his spine, wicked feather like blades rippled in shades of deep blue. J-Dawg's eyes swirled in a mixture of abalone like colors.

"Wow! That's really cool!" Tristan exclaimed. "Hey, do you know how to get outta here?"

"Do ya think I'd be here if I could leave? When Scummy Ball Sack killed Eleanor, I became trapped here," J-Dawg explained, sadness creeped into his tone.

"Who was Eleanor?"

"The witch who lived here. One day, she brought him home, showed him how to use the wards. He killed her." J-Dawg choked up, a crystal tear rolled down his face. "He doesn't know of my existence. He hasn't seen me."

"How long has he been staying here?" inquired Tristan, noticing the perfect crystal slide down to rest on the couch. Nonchalantly, Tristan picked it up, eyeing the prism. He could try to use it to boost a telepathic call to his dad. But he needed to wait until his magic regenerated. The spells he cast for Scott drained his energy.

"Off and on since spring. I've tried to catch him activating the ward, but I can't seem to figure it out," J-Dawg huffed his frustration.

"Do you know where the vessel empowering the ward is located?"

J-Dawg shook his head, dejectedly.

"Well, between the two of us, maybe we can figure it out." *We have to.* Tristan thought silently to himself.

12

"So, I hear you pissed off Marcus Denton, Pacific Northwest Regional Alpha over all the Were clans," Steve Kane observed, as he walked into the Bitterroot River Clan home through the back door.

Surprised, I shrugged my shoulders. "I classify it as a teaching moment. He now realizes a vulnerability exists for Weres in dealing with witches." I explained. Then the thought occurred to me. "How did you hear about it?"

"Denton contacted several covens, trying to hire a witch to cast a protection ward, keeping you out of his clan home. Two different coven leaders called me to inquire about you. I told them I'd worked with you before and given a choice I'd side with you, every time. Anyone who stood against you, isn't someone I'd associate with. I also mentioned it may be difficult to create a ward you wouldn't get through, if you really wanted in."

I laughed. "Thanks for the vote of confidence. By not recognizing a witch can hold their own against a Were, places the Were in grave danger. With a psychopath running around, victimizing unsuspecting Were women, those warnings must go out."

"It appears he received the message. In other, less pleasant news, we believe we located Rosie." Steve sighed. "After performing numerous locate spells focusing on different aspects of her person and aura, Ryan provided us with some of her hair." He inhaled deeply, then exhaled slowly. "We discovered her. Embedded in the middle of a rock cliff over by Painted Rocks Lake, a little southeast of the Bitterroot River Clan home. Just west of Scott's house." Rosie served as the secretary at 3D Investigations prior to her defection with Kiki and Scott. I knew something was off with her. The ward I placed to protect the agency wouldn't allow her to pass through. Ryan and Malachi ignored my warnings. She'd shared information of our investigation with him. Until she got caught.

"That's not too far from here," Devon remarked.

Grimacing, Nate asked, "Embedded?"

Steve nodded. "We assume they attempted to teleport."

"Karma's a bitch. Break a psychopath out of jail, end up a rock. Sorry, I don't have sympathy for anyone who would help a rapist," I stated, bluntly. Her and I never really got along anyway. She nursed a massive crush on Malachi. He barely realized she was live.

"Any sign of Kiki?" Dylan asked.

Shaking his head, Stephen stated, "I'm guessing she suffered the same end as Rosie since there's no sign of her in his house. With their spell books in his possession, it doesn't bode well for Kiki."

Later in the afternoon, I received a call. I didn't recognize the number that appeared on my caller id. Eagerly, I answered it, in hopes it was Tristan. "Shyenne de la Angelino?" A deep male voice inquired.

I replied, hesitantly. "Yes?"

"This is Carlos Rodriguez, Sargent at Arms for the Pacific Northwest Regional Were Clan. You are hereby ordered to appear before Marcus Denton, Pacific Northwest Regional Alpha."

"Why?"

"To answer to the charges of insubordination."

I laughed. "I have to answer to charges of insubordination while he failed to warn the clans that a psychopath preyed on young female Weres in his region? Are you fucking kidding me?"

Apparently, I caught the Sargent at Arms off guard. He stuttered, "No, I'm not kidding. You are required to appear tomorrow morning at nine a.m. at the Clan home in Seattle."

"Oh, for fuck's sake! I am attempting to locate said psychopath as well as my cousin who he kidnapped. I don't have time to deal with an alpha male who's pride got bruised by a witch," I replied angrily.'

"Shyenne. Stop." Bane spoke softly but forcibly.

"Damn it! I need to find Tristan! Not pander to a whiny ass-"

"Shut up." Bane took my phone away from me. "Shyenne will be there first thing in the morning."

Dylan pulled out his cell and dialed a number. I rolled my eyes. "Hey. Shy pissed off the regional alpha and was just ordered to appear at the Seattle clan home tomorrow morning." My kitty senses let me hear Malachi's response.

"What did she do?"

"He didn't believe a witch posed a risk to a Were."

"Oh, fuck."

"She 'ported into the clan home, 'ported him back here and hit him with a sleep spell. Lance 'ported him back and ended up hitting his four bodyguards with a spell, dispelled hers and 'ported back here."

Malachi laughed. "I shouldn't laugh 'cuz this is pretty serious. Ah, shit. Alright, I'll be there first thing in the morning. Is she back at our lodge yet?"

"No. We're still trying different ways of tracking Tristan from the Bitterroot River Clan home."

"Alright. Let me talk to her real quick." Dylan handed me the phone. I glared at him. He ignored my look.

"Hey."

"Babe." Malachi sighed deeply. I knew he was shaking his head.

"I know. I shoulda controlled my mouth and 'porting Denton probably wasn't the best way to make my point. It was highly effective, but probably not the smartest thing I've done lately." I owned up to my shit. "You don't need to come tomorrow. Watching me receive my comeuppance isn't gonna be fun."

"Who's going with you?"

76

"I am." Bane stated.

"Me, too." Jadan replied.

"I'm going." Devon stated.

"I'm coming as well." Lance said.

A chorus of "no" met Lance's comment.

"Shay?"

"No." My brothers and I agreed.

"Alright. I'll be at the Bitterroot River Clan home first thing."

I swear my eyes are going to get stuck in the back of my head because I roll them so much.

Tristan. How to find Tristan? We tried telepathy, running rampant through astral space. What next? Scrying? That sounded like a good next step. "Devon, do you happen to have a map?"

"What kind of a map?"

Shrugging, "Um, the United States, the world? I'm not sure. I want to try scrying for Tristan," I explained.

"I have a bunch of maps for my geography class. I have a map of each continent and the world, along with the United States and the Pacific Northwest," a Were cat of some sort spoke up.

"Colton, grab them, please," Devon replied.

I opened a portal to our cave and picked up a crystal wrapped in copper, on a copper chain. I walked outside to the area I last saw Tristan before Scott kidnapped him. I walked back and forth until I located the spot holding the strongest feel of him. Aware of blood and stomach gore, I dropped to the ground, sitting cross-legged on the grass. Earth magic seeped into my soul as I communed. Colton came out carrying numerous maps.

He handed them to me, then stepped back. "Here ya go."

I took the maps, "Thanks."

Starting with the Pacific Northwest, I laid the map over the spot where Tristan's essence felt the strongest. In my mind, I pictured him, his sweet, laughing, playful smile, unruly blond curls framing his face. Emerald green eyes twinkling. Swirling the crystal above the map, earth magic flowed through me down the chain. But it indicated nothing. I tried the United States map, using small centric circles regionally. Nothing. Each continent and the world maps produced the same result. A big fat zero.

Running my hands through my hair, I racked my brain, for other ways to scry for him. The Weres stayed a safe distance from me, watching my activities. I pulled my phone out and called Al. He picked up instantly. "I'm scrying for Tristan. Can I borrow some of your blood?"

"Blood, typically, isn't necessary for scrying, Shy." Al responded, in his educator's tone.

"I'm not getting any hits using the typical method. I'm hoping if I use your blood, since it's like part of him, it might add more oompf." I explained, twirling a blade of grass between my fingers.

"Okay. Are you still at the Bitterroot River Clan home?"

"Yes. I think it may be stronger to use the last known spot he stood."

Al appeared almost instantly next to me, unmelding from the earth, with Lance behind him. He dropped down beside me. "Do you have a knife?"

"I don't need one," I stated, one of my fingers morphing into a claw, I scratched Al's arm and rubbed the crystal in his blood. I repeated my ministrations with the maps, to no avail. At some point, Bane and Jadan appeared, observing. Huffing in frustration, I choked back a sob, "Any ideas?"

"What if we all help scry? Like a coven scrying?" Jadan suggested, shrugging his shoulders. I was surprised that he was actually participating. He typically ignored or downplayed his magical involvement. Our grandfather hated magic and hated when any of us used it.

"Is that a thing?" Bane asked, scratching his head.

We looked at each other. "I don't think it'll hurt anything," Lance said. "Call Shay and Dylan. With all of us, maybe it provides more power."

"We're all of the same blood, looking for the same blood, that should help, right?" Jadan asked as he called Shay. Bane dialed Dylan.

Within moments, they appeared. We sat in a circle, bringing the same picture of Tristan up in our minds. With our left hand grounded in the dirt, and our right hands joined together wrapped with the copper chain, the crystal swung above the map. Each map. Nothing.

13

Shay and Lance remained at our lodge while the rest of us 'ported to the clan home in Seattle. I dressed for battle: leather and kevlar, my hair pulled back tight, silver spiked arm bracers traveling down my fingers, shin and knee guards, steel toed boots with three-inch silver stiletto heels. We appeared in the chamber room. Malachi, Devon and Jaden sat down in their respective seats. Bane stood behind me, arms crossed. I approached the center of the room. Several other clan leaders took their places. Large vid screens framed the walls. Other alphas appeared via the screens including my grandfather and Kyle McCormack, the Asotin County Clan leader.

"I am Shyenne de la Angelino, Alpha Female of the Salmon River Pride and member of the Nez Perce Coven," extending my arms out. "Here as ordered." I rocked my head back and forth, in a disrespectful manner. Subordination not part of my persona. At all.

"You are charged with insubordination. How do you plead?" Denton questioned, getting straight to the point. He sat at the head of the chambers, wearing a suit, tie and smug look on his face.

Provoke him. Bane 'pathed to me.

I raised an eyebrow in surprise. Typically, Bane counseled me to not pick fights. Especially with "authority" figures. "I plead guilty. You are charged with criminal negligence. How do you plead?"

Astonished by my guile, "Excuse me?" He laughed, turning his head to look at the other alpha males. "Who are you to address me in that manner?"

"Were you not paying attention a moment ago? I am Shyenne de la Angelino, Alpha Female of the Salmon River Pride and member of the Nez Perce Coven. I'm under your protection. You failed to protect the clans under your care by forwarding the warning on to the other clans regarding Scott Clark, the psychopath witch preying upon young Were women. Four women under your protection were kidnapped, raped and tortured by said psychopath. So, how do you plead?"

His anger was almost palpable. "This hearing is to discuss your sentence. You are to be incarcerated in the dungeon here for thirty days. To use as we see fit." The leer in his eyes made me barf in my mouth a little.

Shaking my head, "Yeah, that's not going to work for me. You see, I'm currently involved with finding my cousin and recapturing Scott Clark. What plea did you want to enter regarding your charges?"

"I determine what constitutes a threat to the Weres and didn't feel that the witch was a viable threat," Denton stated flatly. "Now, about-"

Interrupting the asshole, "Devon, if you would have been informed about Clark, what would your response have been?" I questioned the Bitterroot River Clan Heir Apparent.

"I would have ordered the young women who lived alone to come stay at the clan home. We would have provided escorts to and from work and any outings outside of the home."

"Kyle McCormack, what measures did you put in place when Malachi informed you of the risk to young Were women?"

"We sent out an email to all of our members, warning them. All young Were women who lived alone moved into the pride home or moved in with other Weres. A picture of Clark was circulated. We provided escorts within the community."

"Grandfather, when you were informed of the threat posed by Clark, how did you respond?"

"The same as McCormack, with the exception of the escort showing up thirty minutes prior to leaving work to observe any and all questionable interactions that may pose a threat."

"That is a very good idea," Kyle responded, nodding in agreement.

"Yes, it is. After debriefing our women who Clark victimized, having the escort show up early would probably have identified him as a risk in all four circumstances," Devon observed, anger tinting his voice.

"My actions are not up for discussion. We are addressing Shyenne de la Angelino's insubordination." Denton interrupted.

While Denton droned on, I 'pathed to Bane, *How much do you want me to provoke him?*

I want him to challenge you.

Sighing deeply, I trust Bane more than anyone in my life, other than Shay. *Okaaaay.* I interrupted Denton's monologue. "I call for a vote of no confidence in the Pacific Northwest Regional Alpha." That shut him up.

Malachi stood up and stated, "I agree."

Jadan responded, "I agree."

"As do I," Devon replied.

Several other alphas hollered their approval, as well. Denton jumped over the desk, stalking towards me. Bane stepped around me. "I am Bane de la Angelino, Sargent at Arms of the Selway River Pride and the Salmon River Pride. I challenge you for the role of Regional Alpha for the Pacific Northwest Clans."

"Holy shit. I did not see that coming!" I announced, jerking my head back in shock, as if someone struck me. I glanced to Jadan. He appeared as surprised as me. Grandfather looked thrilled, jumping to his feet in his study, waving his cane in the air. Three of Denton's goons backed him up. I pulled *Eadala* as Bane pulled his sword *Sharafina*. His sword is similar to mine, just bigger and heavier, scaled to his size, versus lil ol' me. "How are we doing this, Denton? Are you sending in your Sargent?"

He unknotted the tie at his throat and unbuttoned his jacket. Eyeing both our swords, he nodded. Like the pole vault, I stuck mine into the floor and vaulted over Denton, landing between the goonies. One took off after seeing our weapons. The second parried my first blow, aimed at his head. But not the next, I swirled around, coming up behind him, as I whipped the dull edge of *Eadala* around, taking him out at the knees. He landed hard on the floor, his head bouncing off the marble tile, making a grotesque noise. Instantly, he lost consciousness. Several alphas cheered.

The Sargent was the third man. Within moments, I realized he possessed skills substantially better than the other guy, parrying my blows with his long sword, tossing in a few offensive moves. We danced around, taking turns, attacking, retreating, defending, striking. The sound of metal striking metal reverberated through the room.

The alpha males' seats created a large circle. Plenty of room for two to tango. Our swords sang as we met each other, blow for blow. I began to tire and noticed he slowed as well. I caught his eye, winked and blew him a kiss. My boldness caused him to pause. With a quick flick of my wrist, I caught his blade between two of mine and sent it flying. Jadan caught it. I swept out with my leg, knocking him down on his back and stuck my sharp point to his throat.

"Serve Bane or death. Your choice."

"I'll serve Bane."

Nodding, I allowed him to rise. "Go stand between Jadan and Malachi."

"Remind me to thank Jadan for not allowing me to challenge Shyenne. Holy shit!" I heard my grandfather remark. I smirked. He referred to the incident where he tried to marry me off to Devon, even though I wasn't part of his clan. He and I maintain a very cantankerous relationship. To say the least. I moved to stand behind Bane, using my forearm to wipe sweat from my brow.

Denton pulled a long sword and swung wide towards my brother, which he easily parried. Bane taught me to fight. He played with Denton, allowing him to be the aggressor, blocking each strike. Bane danced, literally danced, around Denton. I giggled. Denton briefly glanced at me, providing Bane the opportunity he wanted. He quickly advanced, swinging his sword, *Sharafina*. Honor. Something Denton knew nothing about. Using short, quick rotations, each end challenged Denton. He parried the first three thrusts. Sweat poured from his brow, as he backpedaled.

Reaching the chamber seats, Denton vaulted on top of the table, then jumped to the other side. Easily leaping over the table, Bane pursued his prey, swinging at him while flying through the air. Denton fell against the carpet and rolled to the side as Bane swung down. Denton scrambled to his feet, backed up against the wall. The seated alphas leapt over the table, clearing the way. Denton threw chairs at Bane. Instead of hurdling them or knocking them out of the way, Bane jumped upon the table, advancing on Denton. The Regional Alpha swung recklessly towards Bane's legs. He easily blocked the blow, banging Denton's sword and hand hard against the wall. Bones cracked at the impact. Holding his hand, Denton raced back through the tangle of chairs. Bane waited patiently atop the table. It wasn't like Denton could leave. The observers made sure to stay away from the singing blades. Denton placed a good amount of space between himself and Bane, heaving deep breaths. The realization he wouldn't win this battle, crossed Denton's face as he made his way back into the center.

Bane watched him buy time to catch his breath. Use to intense sparring matches with Jadan and I, Bane's heartbeat barely rose, his breathing unlabored and his body had yet to perspire. Flipping from the table, Bane landed in front of Denton, sweeping his feet out from under him. Denton fell back and rolled over several times, jumping to his feet as Bane thrust down, barely missing him. Swinging, Denton hit Bane in the thigh, drawing blood. I inhaled sharply. It took all of my self-control not to jump in to aid my brother, but I knew the rules of engagement. Bane had to conquer him. On his own.

Play time was over. Double handed, Bane instituted the move he called the windmill, spinning *Sharafina* rapidly, changing the elevation of the weapon as he bore down on Denton. As Denton went high, defending his head, Bane struck low, cutting his legs off at the knees. Blood sprayed everywhere. Falling to the floor, his sword fell next to him. Bane kicked it towards me. I picked it up and threw it to Jadan. *Sharafina* lay against his neck.

"Death or exile?" Bane offered Denton.

Pain and shock overcame Denton. He passed out. Rolling his eyes, Bane turned towards the alphas. The alpha peanut gallery began chanting, "Death!"

He turned to me, I replied, "There is no honor in killing an unconscious man."

"Agreed." Jadan stated. Wow. We agreed on something?

"I propose I heal him and teleport him to… Iceland? Russia? Antarctica?" I stated, thinking someplace far away and cold.

Several alphas groaned. Someone muttered, "Weak hearted."

Swinging around, "It takes no strength, guile or honor to kill a comatose man. He deserves better. Even though I disagree with most of his actions and policies, he is an alpha and earned his way to this station. He deserves to be treated in an honorable manner," I retorted, standing beside Bane.

Nodding, "I agree. Heal him. Take him to… Russia?" Bane decreed.

I dropped to one knee, showing deference and legitimizing Bane's claim to the … alphaship? "As you wish, Regional Alpha for the Pacific Northwest Were Clans," I stated, bowing. Bane is the only person I can honestly say I'd ever voluntarily bow down to.

Jadan jumped over the table and knelt next to me, acquiescing to Bane's appointment. Malachi followed suit with Devon falling beside him. Grandfather knelt down, as did all the other alphas, in turn.

"Will you be taking over the Sea-Tac Clan?" The Sargent at Arms asked, as Denton had served as alpha for the local group.

Shaking his head, "Fuck, no."

"Bane will return to the Clearwater Pride," grandfather announced, grandly via vid screen.

"I offer a place within our clan. We have the ice cream rooms." Devon tempted Bane with a lopsided smile.

Hesitating a moment, I suggested, "Hang with the Salmon River Pride. I'll give you the miner's cabin and homestead." I almost felt guilty, knowing my brother better than anyone else.

Bane pointed at me, "Sold!"

Smiling, I walked to Denton and placed the cleanly split limbs where they belonged. I performed several healing spells, boosting his own regeneration abilities, allowing him to heal, affixing his legs back together, before he bled to death. Several gasps reached my ears from the alphas, unaware of my abilities.

"Shy, go find Tristan. Jadan and I will teleport Denton." Bane stated, standing next to me as I finished providing care.

Nodding, I saluted. My bullshit-o-meter reached over flowing with this political crap. I just wanted to find my cousin. I 'ported out and returned to the Bitterroot River Clan Home.

14

I stood in the yard at the Bitterroot River Clan home, surrounded by pine trees and mountains. The deep blue sky stretched above me. The potent fragrance of the headwaters of the Selway River just miles away, as the crow flies, teased my nostrils. Closing my eyes, I searched for Tristan. My mind stretched, reaching, seeking the elements I recognized as my cousin. But I found nothing.

Inhaling deeply, I exhaled slowly, frustrated. Scott Clark. How could I track that fucking prick? I knew the Orchards Coven performed searches for him on a frequent basis, to no avail. They were familiar with his magic and used the knowledge in their search spells. What did I have access to they didn't?

A totally gross thought entered my mind. I knew the location of his entrails, bodily fluids, and, barfing a little, the lower part of his arm. Using these parts of his body, could I find Scott? I contemplated the idea. No one cleaned his house yet, as it remained an active crime scene. Ravalli County Sheriff's Department continued to investigate the house and property. Fluids lingered on site, sunk into the earth. I didn't know where his arm was, but assumed the detectives could point me in the right direction. No pun intended.

Using any part of his body provided me with DNA, chromosomes, genetic material, items completely specific to him and him alone. Even if he healed, if he regenerated, the ... pieces ... would contain the genetic information specific only to him. I contemplated my options. The arm. It would not be the same as whatever may regenerate. Injuries, usage, life would have affected the …portion left behind. When the limb regenerated, it would only possess the DNA, not the effects of life. Entrails. Bile rose up in my throat. I considered this option. Whatever food, liquids, substances he ingested tainted his guts.

Sighing dejectedly, I pondered his blood. It flowed freely into the earth. Removing the earth would actually be fairly simple. While all kinds of things influenced and affected blood, overall, I figured it remained fairly consistent. He didn't suffer from a disease. That I knew of. I grimaced. What a fuck head. Pulling out my phone, I called Shay, then conferenced in Lance.

"We're actually sitting next to each other in the library at our house," Shay commented, drily.

"Well, then, one of you hang up. What do you think of doing a locate spell on Scott's blood? I think we could remove the earth from where I eviscerated him."

Silence met my suggestion.

"Hello?"

"Give us a moment. We're digesting, contemplating, barfing at your suggestion." Lance retorted.

I rolled my eyes, even though my action went unnoticed. The two mumbled between themselves but I couldn't really make out anything sensible.

After a few moments, "We can't come up with any reason why that won't work." Lance remarked. Again, I rolled my eyes, even though they kind of agreed with me.

"I don't know if the sheriff's department is still on site. Let's wait until dark and 'port up there. We can separate the blood from the earth. Let's try to perform a locate spell using his blood to find them."

After dark, Lance and I 'ported to Scott's house. At the site where I released his guts from his abdomen, we extracted the coagulated blood from the soil and placed it into a glass bottle. Then, we returned to the Bitterroot River Clan home. Sitting in the yard with the maps, I rubbed my scrying crystal into Scott's blood, coating it liberally. One by one, I twirled my oogy encrusted crystal over each map. To no avail.

15

While Scott slept fitfully, Tristan and J-Dawg searched in vain for the ward. They cleared the kitchen with Tristan discovering no further food stores. A whimper emanated from the couch.

"Scummy Ball Sack rises," J-Dawg remarked dryly, hooking a thumb towards the couch.

"How ya feelin'?" Tristan inquired, shooting the little dragon a look.

"Like some cunt cut off my arm and disemboweled me," pain etched deep in Scott's tone. "Can you help me up, please?"

"Sure," Tristan left the kitchen, moving towards the couch. "I just finished cleaning the kitchen. Our food situation is actually quite dire." Reaching down, Tristan grasped Scott's hand, helping him to stand on his feet. "Dude! You're on fire! That's not good!"

"Yeah, it is. It's wonderful! Just what Scummy Ball Sack deserves!" J-Dawg cheered, waving his arms around.

Tristan rolled his eyes as he assisted Scott to the bathroom. "Why isn't your healing ring activated?"

Drowning in pain, his voice scarcely a whisper, "Activated? Doesn't it work… automatically?" Scott ended, barely making a sound, as he crossed into the bathroom.

"Uh, obviously not. You're not healing outside of the spell I cast, from the looks of you." Tristan pointed out.

"Why in the hell would you heal this piece of squid shit?" J-Dawg demanded, hands on his hips, hovering on the opposite side of Scott, sticking his tongue out at him.

Tristan shot a deadly look towards J-Dawg. "If you die, I might die. I can't get passed the ward. Very little food remains in the kitchen. Enough for mere days. You need help, more than I can provide. We need food. Tell me how to 'port through the ward. I'll bring back medical help," Tristan implored Scott.

"From your fucking cousin who did this to me? No thanks," Scott whimpered as he finished up in the bathroom.

"Hell, I'll contact your sister, your mom! Anyone you want! I can 'port to them and 'port back, immediately." Tristan aided Scott back to the couch, easing him down. "Without help, you're going to die. I don't possess the ability to provide the amount of healing you require."

Time passed slowly as Scott tried to catch his breath, overcome with pain. Sweat beaded his brow. "How do I activate the ring?" He ignored Tristan's offer of help.

Tristan shrugged his shoulders, running a hand through his hair, frustrated. "It could be a word, a thought, an action."

Scott recounted a deluge of magical words, trying to trigger the ring. When that failed to work, he performed a series of single hand gestures. Silently, he attempted to initiate the healing process through thought. Tristan watched his machinations apprehensively.

"Dammit!" Scott studied Tristan. His features twisted harsh with pain. "Can you create a healing potion?"

He concealed his relief when Scott failed to activate the healing ring. "With access to the ingredients, I can make an 'okay' potion. But I haven't seen any spell components or potion ingredients in my search for food. Unless you know a spell utilizing mustard and horseradish." Tristan pointed out, raising an eyebrow. "I can hit ya with another healing spell but I don't think it will be too effective, at this point. Want me to clean up the wound and re-bandage it for you?"

Scott hesitated, then nodded. Tristan fetched the hydrogen peroxide and gauze from the bathroom. Carefully, he pulled the bandage off. Ooze, blood and goo of a greenish tint soaked through. Scott whimpered as Tristan exposed the wound to the air.

"That is grosser than donkey diarrhea!" Hovering behind Tristan, watching his ministrations, J-Dawg started dry-heaving. "Uh, I'm gonna blow chunks!"

"Dragon puke will not help the situation," Tristan retorted, as he tried to clean the injury as thoroughly as possible.

"No kind of puke will be helpful," Scott responded, grimacing in pain.

Tristan choked back his laughter, as the little dragon continued to dry heave. "Oh my gods! I didn't know human intestines looked like that! Are they supposed to be blackish?"

"I'll cast a healing spell directly into the wounded area. Perhaps that will provide the best effect with our limited resources." Tristan performed the healing. The color improved, with the signs of infection partially subsiding. "Dude. I don't believe I can provide enough healing power before your injuries kill you. I'm not strong enough. You're going to die of infection and I'm going to starve to death." Tristan stated bluntly, meeting Scott's gaze.

"Hit me with a sleep spell."

"Let me hit him with a chair! Scummy Ball Sack with donkey diarrhea infection!" J-Dawg suggested, bopping around, fists raised.

Tristan knocked him out, then turned his attention to the young dragon. "If he dies, I'll probably die. There isn't enough food here. My family might not find me before I starve to death. We must find that damn ward!" The next morning, Tristan and his trusty sidekick, J-Dawg, searched the perimeter and kitchen once again, still failing to locate the ward.

Overnight Tristan's magic regenerated.

"I want to try to use the crystal from your tear to send my dad a telepathic message. If I'm standing on the earth and focus my magic through the crystal, it should boost the range, hopefully reaching him." Tristan explained to J-Dawg, holding the crystal between his fingers.

J-Dawg punched the air, "Sounds like a plan! Let's do this!" He flew behind Tristan as he exited the cottage.

Sitting on the steps of the porch, Tristan took off his socks and shoes. Burying his toes into the lush grass, he grounded himself. Holding the crystal between his thumb and pointer finger, he focused his psionic magic through the crystal, searching for his father. *Dad!* Nothing.

Frustrated, Tristan ran his hand through his tousled hair, J-Dawg mimicked the action. A thought occurred to him. "Where did Eleanor practice her magic?" Tristan asked, turning to face J-Dawg as he hovered above the steps.

J-Dawg hesitated to answer the question. Tristan gazed at him expectantly. After numerous moments, the little dragon appeared to reach a decision. "She set her altar upstairs in the attic. It's not easy to access. I teleport through the ceiling. Eleanor never revealed her magic room to Scummy Ball Sack."

"I can teleport. Lead the way." They entered astral space and 'ported to the hidden room.

"Scummy Ball Sack never found this room," J-Dawg stated as Tristan looked around. Very little light leaked into the attic through a small circular window. With a flick of his paw, J-Dawg illuminated the area. A row of magic books lined one wall. An altar stood in the center of the room, covered with a green velvet cloth. An array of candles, in varying degrees of use, bordered the edges. A shelf held an assortment of glass bottles and vials with a variety of ingredients available for potions, charms and spell casting.

J-Dawg plopped down on a deep purple cushion in the corner. "Are you going to create a healing potion for Scummy Ball Sack?" J-Dawg asked belligerently, as he kneaded the pillow, fluffing his scales.

"Nope. I'll try to keep him alive until we find a way out of here. But my best chance of surviving him is to ensure he remains weak," Tristan remarked as he created a mental inventory of the bottles, noting numerous ingredients could be used for food. He could create one hell of a flavorful soup. After a few moments, he moved to the bookshelf, perusing the titles.

He spent several hours reading spells from the books, hoping for anything that might aid him in dropping the ward.

Meanwhile, J-Dawg snored loudly from his pillow, then slowly stretched, waking up. "Did you find anything helpful?"

Shaking his head, "I'm too weak a witch to cast anything remotely powerful enough to make it through the barrier." Tristan sighed as he laid the book down he thumbed through.

"Steal Scummy Ball Sack's magic."

Tristan started to respond, then stopped, considering the little dragon's suggestion. "I could go in astrally and look at his magic. See what his set up is like. I don't know if I'd know what to do." As he contemplated the idea, he realized this may be the best option. His only option to escape.

"I do."

"You do what?" Tristan responded vaguely as he considered the possibility.

"I know how to transfer the magic," J-Dawg replied. "Or at least, I saw how he stole Eleanor's magic before he killed her."

"No shit?" Surprised, Tristan felt a spark of hope flare. "Fantastic! Let's check it out." They ported back down into the kitchen. Scott stirred on the couch, moaning in pain. Tristan paused, waiting to see if he woke or returned to an unconscious state. He opened his eyes.

Tristan sighed. "Hey, Dude. How ya' feelin'?"

"Like shit." Beads of perspiration covered his brow and drenched the blanket covering him.

"I think you have a fever again." Tristan noted, touching his foot. Heat radiated from his body. "Tell me how to get through the ward. I'll find your mom. She's a great healer."

Struggling to sit up, Scott shook his head. "Help me up." Tristan aided him to his feet. "I'm going to take a shower. Can you fix me something to eat?"

Tristan nodded and entered the kitchen as Scott stumbled unevenly towards the bathroom. The water came on in the shower as he opened a can of soup, dumped it into a pot and set it on the stove for Scott. He found a can of chili for himself. Two cans of food remained in the cupboard. He vacillated between adding more water to both, making the food stores last longer, or running out of food sooner, forcing Scott to release the ward. Sighing heavily, he turned the faucet off. Scott took a very quick shower, returning to the couch, obviously in severe pain. He'd removed the bandage.

"Holy polka dot ant-eaters from Mars! His belly looks awful! I'm seriously gonna barf!" J-Dawg flew to the kitchen and hurled into the garbage can.

Rolling his eyes, Tristan turned and observed Scott. The wound oozed green pus. A small area of the injury appeared blackened.

"Ah, shit. Scott. Let me bring your mom here."

"Can you get me a petal from a pine cone? I want to try to put a healing spell in a charm," Scott gasped as he eased back onto the couch. "I can't directly heal myself but I can through a charm or potion."

Tristan hesitated briefly, then wordlessly, went outside and picked up a pine cone, pulling off one of the petals. Returning to the house, he handed it over. He doubted Scott possessed enough energy to cast the spell. Moments later proved him correct. Scott threw the petal down in frustration. Tristan poured hydrogen peroxide over the wound as Scott screamed. Then placed gauze over it.

"Scott, that's the last of the peroxide. There's nothing else to use as an antiseptic. There's enough food for one more meal. You are not healing. You developed a severe infection. Your magic is not regenerating because your body is utilizing all your energy to fight your injuries. We are both going to die here if you don't let me past the ward." Tristan tried to convince him.

Shaking his head, Scott drank the split pea soup directly from the bowl. After he gulped it down, he stared wordlessly into the bowl, weighing his options. "Transfer some of your magical energy to me and I'll cast the healing spell into the charm."

"No." Tristan stated bluntly.

"It appears we've reached an impasse." Tristan nodded. "Will you cast a healing spell and a sleep spell?" Tristan nodded and cast the two spells.

Scott instantly fell into unconsciousness.

"What an asshole. He'd rather kill us both than release me." Tristan sighed heavily, running a hand through his hair as he stared down at Scott's prone figure. J-Dawg mirrored his action. Tristan rolled his eyes. "Alright. I'll go in psionically and check out his magic center. Watch over me. Call to me astrally if anything untoward occurs out here. He should be out for several hours."

J-Dawg snapped a salute and pantomimed walking a watch guard route in midair over Scott. "I'm going to give myself a headache rolling my eyes so much," Tristan stated sardonically as he sank into the green Lazy Boy chair. He relaxed his body and entered a meditative state, floating into astral space. He entered Scott's being and wandered around. Uncommon in most witches, psionic abilities ran strong in the Nez Perce Coven. Tristan's abilities didn't compare to Lance, Shy or Shay's, but what he lacked in ability, he made up for in knowledge. Immediately, he recognized substantial differences in the make-up of a "normal" witch brain and Scott's. *I wonder if these differences can be attributed to his psychopathology? Or if his psychopathology can be attributed to these differences?* He studied the cerebral cortex and the amygdala, noticing a lack of connections relating to empathy and decision making. In fact, the two sections appeared to barely communicate with each other. This was vastly different than he observed in his cousins. Tristan noted his observations, knowing his father would be very interested in the obvious differences, especially with Scott's proclivities.

He continued to wander through Scott's brain until he reached the magic center. This too, appeared quite different than a typical witch. His magic lay in three separate sections. One piece embedded in his brain. The other two seemed to rest on top of the area, not actively partaking of the energy, not even a fragment of his own magic. He had not incorporated his father's transferred magic, or Eleanor's stolen magic, into his own. *Their magic would be easier to transfer from his being since it hasn't been assimilated.* Tristan surmised. *Now, how?*

Studying the two masses, he tried to identify which belonged to who. His father practiced fire magic, too, meaning his magic should resemble Scott's. Closely comparing them, he found the flame at the core of one mass and the matching flame at the center of Scott's own magic. When Kiki aided him to break out of jail, she provided him a crystal his father used to transfer his magic to him. But he failed to incorporate his father's magic into his own. By default, that meant the other mass must belong to Eleanor. He couldn't recognize the type of magic based on observation but her books in her altar room appeared to focus on light magic.

Completely unfamiliar with light magic, he learned a lot today, reading through her tomes. He believed himself to be well educated regarding the magic disciplines. But light magic seemed rather unique. It dealt with manipulating light to achieve the desired results.

Neither mass demonstrated any attachment to Scott's psyche. Tristan didn't even see a tether linking the magics. They seemed to just... lie there. Richard's magic barely glowed, compared to Scott's. But his magic didn't look very healthy, either. The strands waved listlessly. The center flame glowed a dull red color with a spot of yellow in the center. Richard's barely emanated a red hue, mostly gray. Only a few tendrils waved about. Most seemed to barely float.

Eleanor's magic appeared even weaker. Very little light radiated from the center, almost like it may blink out at any moment. *It doesn't look like the transferred magics are receiving nutrients from his body. Since he failed to fully integrate them into his own, they aren't being nourished.*

How would he... move them? He studied the areas. Psionically, he "poked" Eleanor's magic. The motion reverberated across it. *I can move it that easily?* As he considered the possibilities, he thought about when Shyenne removed some of her Were essence to use in the healing potion for Scott's sister, Kayla.

Shyenne scooped some up and kept it in astral space until she incorporated it into the potion. If Tristan picked up the magic and moved it from Scott to himself, psionically, and then... mixed it? With his? Scratching his head, Tristan considered the possibility. He hesitated to just willy nilly take the magic. *If I could attempt a transfer on someone. Put Eleanor's magic in J-Dawg? They practiced the same type of magic. I know less about dragon magic than I do about transferring magic. But hypothetically, it should be the same, or at least similar. Right?*

Tristan eased out psionically, entering astral space and then returned to his body. J-Dawg laid along the back of the couch. He jumped up as Tristan opened his eyes. "Geez! You left for a really long time! I worried about you!" Apprehension flowed off the little dragon as his color faded from plum to lavender, in relief.

"How long was I gone?"

"About two hours. Did you find what you searched for?"

Tristan nodded his head. "Did you and Eleanor practice the same type of magic?"

"Yes. She was teaching me new spells. Once I grow up, I would have surpassed her abilities but would be able to assist her," J-Dawg replied, tearfully, as crystals flowed down his cheeks. "She raised me from a hatchling."

"You served as her familiar." J-Dawg nodded. "Is it okay if I check out your magic center?"

He looked confused. "Does it hurt?" He asked timidly.

Tristan shook his head. "You won't even know I'm there," he promised.

"Will it take two hours?"

Tristan laughed. "I don't think so. I want to see if yours is similar to a witch's."

Hesitating, J-Dawg nodded. Tristan followed the same protocol and entered into J-Dawg's mind. His brain appeared similar, but different than a witch. Instead of studying and identifying the differences, Tristan searched for his magic. He found it, rather quickly, as its location lay in the same place as typical. His magic center glowed with immense potential, but limited activity. Shining light surrounded it. It appeared similar, but different from Eleanor's. As Tristan studied it closer, he noticed intertwined fibers made up the magic. *If I weave the strands from his magic into the fibers of hers, perhaps that would incorporate the two.* Tristan observed the area intently, fairly certain this plan would work. The base of the magic sank into J-Dawg's psyche, forming a strong foundation. He recalled that Eleanor and Richard's magics laid upon the psyche, failing to take root. He eased out of J-Dawg and back into his own body.

"I think I have a plan."

16

"How did Scott take Eleanor's magic?" Tristan asked J-Dawg as they ate pancakes while watching one of J-Dawg's favorite cartoons starring ADHD mouse looking characters.

"Reading from his spell book, he transferred her magic into a crystal. Then he changed some of the words around and transferred it from the crystal to himself," the little dragon stated, forking a bite of pancake topped with honey drizzled grasshoppers in his mouth. "If I try hard, I can remember all the words."

Tristan contemplated J-Dawg's offer. "I think I'm going to have a better chance of success if I perform the transfer psionically rather than a spell." Hesitating briefly, "I want to try to transfer Eleanor's magic to you and incorporate it into your own."

J-Dawg looked blankly at Tristan for a number of moments, then responded, "Okaaaay."

"Tell me about you, J-Dawg, about light dragons. Do you know where your species originated?" Tristan asked, forking a bite of honey soaked pancake sans grasshoppers into his mouth.

"Yes, we're hatched with the memories, magic and instincts learned by our ancestors. I'm kind of a genetic experiment, you could say. In the Northern Philippines, the Ilokano believe in numerous gods and magical beings. One such being is called an Olimaw. She's a gigantic phantom dragon who swallows the moon." J-Dawg picked up a grasshopper in his talons, swirled it through the honey and popped it into his mouth.

"A local shaman wanted to see if she could design little dragons. She enslaved a Lambana, a small fairy-like creature with dragonfly wings." J-Dawg flapped his iridescent appendages. "Lambanas, renowned for their trickster's personality, desire freedom in nature, above all else.

"After ensnaring a Lambana, the shaman promised him freedom if he mated with Olimaw, stole the clutch of eggs and gave them to her. Using his skills of illusion, the Lambana disguised himself as a sun dragon. On the night of a lunar eclipse, after Olimaw swallowed the moon, the Lambana courted Olimaw with fermented coconut water. The two spent the night entwined amongst the stars." J-Dawg recounted in a singsong voice, rolling his eyes. Tristan hid a smirk. "Olimaw laid her eggs within the Milky Way. Once she fell asleep," talking from the side of his mouth, conspiratorially, "passed out more likely, Lambana grabbed the eggs and handed them over to the shaman, who freed him."

The tiny dragon popped another honey soaked grasshopper into his mouth. "As you can imagine, Olimaw awoke with a nasty hangover, feeling horribly bloated and instantly missed her eggs. She failed to find the sun dragon anywhere. But she remembered his scent. Sniffing him out, she discovered the Lambana. As soon as he saw her, he confessed everything, fearing her retribution. Angry with the shaman for enslaving him in the first place, he told Olimaw where to find her." J-Dawg took a moment to fork another bite, savoring the honey-soaked grasshopper. "Hearing Olimaw's might rooaaar of rage," the little dragon roared, "the shaman fled the island. With the eggs. She trotted around the globe, selling them to witches, sorcerers, shamans, clerics, druids, demons – any magic user with money, items of value or magic to trade. Olimaw chases her still. She checks on each hatchling, ensuring their safety and care. If she feels the hatchling is mistreated, Olimaw returns them to the Philippines."

Tristan blinked in amazement at J-Dawg's story of his family history. "Wow." After processing the information a few moments longer, he asked, "Has she checked on you?"

J-Dawg shook his head. "I hear my brothers and sisters thoughts. We converse a lot. I've told my hatchlings all about you. Since your arrival, I moved down on Olimaw's list. Several of my hatchlings suffer in dangerous situations. I told Olimaw I'm safe here with you."

The stamp of mini-dragon approval. Great, Tristan thought to himself. "Does she think she can break through the ward?"

"She says no one can cast a spell to keep her away from her babies," J-Dawg pronounced.

"Yep, sounds like a mom."

17

Contemplating what he was about to do, Tristan decided to formulate a plan rather than recklessly attempt to procure the stolen magic from Scott. Astrally, he entered Scott's magic center. Compared to the other two, Eleanor's light magic glowed like a beacon. It lay next to Scott's and his father's but didn't touch. Single tendrils stretched out from the area, reaching towards the other two magic sites. Moving closer, Tristan picked out individual strands making up the bright orb. The longer he observed, he noticed thin long rope like structures intertwined and wound around, entangling, weaving, forming the magic. As he studied the nucleus, the strands became more dense, forming a thicker body. At the center, magic glowed, like a light or an illuminated star, creating the magic. But the base looked thin, barely a foundation. The tendrils weaved about weakly.

Tristan turned his attention to Richard's magic. Flames burned weakly from the nucleus with strings of fire waving around. Individual strands circulated through the area like fire along a line of gunpowder. Similar to Eleanor's, the single pieces intertwined and formed a cohesive ... object? Moving closer, Tristan felt no actual heat emanating from the blaze. As with Eleanor's magic, Richard's lay on top of the psyche, not burrowing down. The individual strands also appeared weak.

Gingerly, he reached out and touched a wicked looking strand reaching towards Scott's magic center. The strand sensed his presence and almost cobra-like it swayed near his hand. Waving his fingers, the string followed him. It performed complex movements, almost as if intelligence imbued it somehow. Suddenly, it whipped out, wrapping around his finger. Tristan fought the urge to jump back from the flame. It didn't burn. Psionically, he touched the strand. Liquid knowledge. It told him how to create flame. He understood it longed for growth, to share, to learn. It hungered. Since the strand wasn't embedded or incorporated into the existing magic site, it wasn't receiving full power, sustenance, the necessary amino acids, nutrients, hormones to feed and nurture the magic. Tendrils reached towards Scott's magic center, but without energy, the magic was dying. Most of Scott's energy strove to fight off the infection ravaging his body. Tristan passed on some nutrients to strand, then unwrapped it from his finger.

He gazed at Scott's magic. It appeared much healthier than the other two but not as strong as it could be. It rested upon a thick foundation, embedded in his psyche. The individual strands weaved about stronger than the other two, but still much weaker than Tristan expected. He attributed it to his injuries. While his body fought to heal wounds, it robbed needed nutrients from his magic. Feeling more confident about the intended transplant, Tristan vacated Scott's mind and entered into astral space.

Moving to J-Dawg's mind, he found his magic and studied it. It too, seemed comprised of multiple individual strands intertwined forming a cohesive body. These strands appeared more robust, thicker, energetic. Weaving around, giving off a spectacular light, they intermingled, forming new strands. One slinked towards Tristan. He let it touch his finger. It explained how to use light to ... move? Not all the concepts made sense. Tristan pulled back. He studied the "root" of the magic. It sank into the psyche. *The individual strands seem to want to grasp on to others. Could I take Eleanor's and allow the strands to intertwine with J-Dawg's? Braid them together?*

Tristan scratched his head. Seemed plausible. Perhaps, Eleanor's library might hold some information. Tristan returned to himself.

"Geez! I thought you were dead! What the hell? I've been trying to wake you up!" Scott wailed, pain edged into his voice, a clammy sweat covered his face.

"Totally exhausted and severely lacking in nutrition, Dude. What's up?"

Scott sighed heavily. "Help me up. I need to take a piss."

Hopping up too quickly, Tristan swayed, dizzy. "I need food." Flopping back down, Tristan slowly gained his feet again, with Scott closely watching his actions.

He assisted Scott to stand and walk into the bathroom. Tristan ran a shaky hand through his hair. *I'll need to cast a sleep spell on him when I do anymore psionic activities. I'll probably have to leave him out once I remove Eleanor's magic. I can't risk him discovering my activities and attempting to stop me. Though I doubt if he could.*

The toilet flushed and Scott opened the door. "There's no food left?"

Shaking his head, Tristan responded. "Only water and flour. I can make bread, pancake tortilla things, but there's nothing else. With random spices I can make water taste good but there's no significant nutritional value. There's dandelions in the yard I can use to make a salad with pine nuts. I can scavenge some worms and grubs. Maybe some bird eggs or a squirrel." Tristan offered, not entirely sure if he was kidding or not. "Let me go get your mom. She can heal you. Your infection is obviously progressing. The stench coming from you is almost over-powering."

In a sudden move, Scott grabbed Tristan's arm and tried to take magic energy from him. Tristan shoved him hard into the wall and he slid down to the floor. "Not cool, Dude. I'm not giving you my power. You tell me how to get past the ward. I guarantee, you'll die before me. I'm sure my family will find me soon."

"Help me up."

Laughing, "Fuck you. You just attacked me. My goodwill expired. You're on your own." Tristan stated, flatly, turning away from Scott.

"'Bout time you told Scummy Ball Sack off."

At some point, Scott semi-crawled to the couch and somehow managed to climb on it. He passed out, probably due to pain. Tristan cast a sleep spell on him, then entered astral space and slipped into his mind. He reached out to Eleanor's magic. Gingerly, he placed his hands under the orb and lifted it. A few tendrils had sunk down into the psyche, but easily pulled up with minimal force. Tristan carried the magic center into astral space and then transferred to J-Dawg. Carefully, he butted it up right next to J-Dawg's glowing orb. Holding out the weakened strings, J-Dawg's healthy strands enthusiastically wrapped around them, diving between them, invading the orb, assimilating it quickly into his own, feeding the nutrient starved areas. As the individual tendrils gained strength, they wrapped and intertwined, quickly melding, forming one main body. The thin, weak strands flourished in front of his eyes, bulking up, becoming more energetic. Some twisted around the base, tunneling into the psyche, eagerly seeking out nutrients. Standing back and surveying his handiwork, the witch's magic center quickly integrated into the dragon's. It appeared now, as one magic. Tristan 'ported to astral space and then returned to the living room.

J-Dawg slept on the back of Tristan's chair. "Yo, J-Dawg! Rise and shine, buddy! No pun intended." Stretching and yawning widely, J-Dawg sat up. "How ya feeling, lil Dude?"

He cocked his head, shrugged his shoulders, "Brighter?"

Tristan smiled. "Try to make a light," he suggested.

A blinding light burst from his paw, hurting Tristan's eyes. "Turn it off!"

J-Dawg extinguished it. "Dammmmnn brah! That was way bright! That's new!"

"No kidding! We may need to practice controlling the brightness. Get you a dimmer switch!" Tristan joked. "Try to 'port through the ward."

J-Dawg jumped to astral space, then returned, almost instantly, shaking his head.

"Detect magic in the kitchen. Let's see if you can find the vessel." They went through all the cupboards and drawers, then moved into the living room, attic and every other room in the house. J-Dawg identified numerous magical items or items magic had been cast upon. But none proved to hold the ward.

Tristan thought for a moment. "Let's go outside by the edge of the barrier." Tristan opened the door and walked out with J-Dawg flying behind him. "Try to dispel the ward."

Concentrating, J-Dawg sent a stream of magic to the barrier. It shimmered slightly, but held. Next, he formed a small ball of light and held it between his two fingers and thumb, gripping it with his talons. He threw it. A high pitched, ear splitting, bunny rabbit death screech emanated from the impact. Tristan and J-Dawg dropped to the ground, as the reverberations echoed the hideous noise. Several seconds after it ended, Tristan cautiously popped his head up, glancing askance at J-Dawg.

Shaking his head, "I won't try that again."

"Good idea. Wade through Eleanor's magic. See if you can find the password for the barrier." Tristan suggested, sticking a finger in each ear, checking for bleeding.

Scratching his head, J-Dawg appeared to be thinking. "Open Sesame! Abracadabra! Hocus Pocus! Amuck, amuck, amuck!"

With a sardonic look, Tristan gazed at the little dragon. "You really thought that would work?"

He shrugged his shoulders, "It would have been cool if it did!"

Tristan sighed. "WWSD?"

"Huh?"

"What would Shy do? She'd think outta the box."

"We're not in a box. It's a sphere. No, not a sphere, a dome. Yeah, I'm going with dome," J-Dawg decided, nodding his head, studying the barrier surrounding them.

Tristan rolled his eyes as he contemplated magical possibilities. "Form a small protective sphere." J-Dawg cast an orb in his paw. "Enlarge it to encompass us."

"Like a snow globe?" J-Dawg inquired. Tristan nodded. J-Dawg expanded it to include them, adding falling snow. Tristan glared at him. The snow stopped.

"Okay, now feed more magic into it, increasing its ability to protect us." As power poured into the orb, "Let it intersect with the barrier. Terrific! Push your barrier through the dome."

J-Dawg focused on his snow globe, re-enforcing the wall as it pressed against the ward. Pulling power from the combined magics, he pushed it gently, yet firmly. Ripples formed in the ward. Waves rolled out from the impact point. The little dragon fed more energy into his barrier, causing the waves to grow. A bubble formed where the two walls intersected, J-Dawg's pushing past the ward. Suddenly, the ward slurped up the barrier created by the dragon, and his protective dome disappeared.

"Did the ward just eat your snow globe?"

"The ward just ate my snow globe."

"Damn."

18

𝔐y phone began playing Nickleback's *Rockstar*. I stepped out of the great room into the backyard, perching on the picnic table.

"I'm trying to surprise you. Where the hell are you?" Malachi demanded, a little huffy.

"The Bitterroot River Clan home." I knew the answer wouldn't please him.

Silent for several long moments, "Why the fuck are you still there?" He asked quietly. "You found the missing women."

"Uh, gee, because that psychopath kidnapped my cousin from this very location! Every attempt I make to find him involves the last known place he stood!" I never pretend to control my temper. "My life isn't returning to normal until I find Tristan!"

"Tristan will show up at his dad's house or our lodge," Malachi tried to console me.

"If he breaks free. Thus far, he hasn't. And I refuse to give up looking for him."

Malachi breathed loudly into the phone.

"You'll love the ice cream rooms here in the Bitterroot." By the time I described the three options, I knew Malachi was hard.

After we hung up, I went in search of Devon. He sat behind a large mahogany desk in his study, reviewing a multitude of papers covered in numbers. I lack the ability to comprehend numbers, literally. Since Shay and I didn't transform to humans until early adolescence, our education regarding mathematics started late. Shay threw herself into catching up. I ran the opposite direction as fast as possible.

"Hi, gorgeous! What's up? Here for a nooner?"

I laughed and gave him a cautious look. "Malachi has a few days off from his tour. I refuse to leave your place," A big shit eating grin spread across Devon's face, "because I haven't found Tristan yet." His smile faded somewhat. "So, I invited him here, describing the ice cream rooms to him."

Devon sat back in his chair, contemplating me, wordlessly. "Pick two or three more women. Reserve the Rocky Road room for all of us."

"All of us?"

"You, me, Malachi and the two to three women."

Surprise flew across his face as a wicked grin slowly replaced it. "Malachi agreed to this?"

I laughed. "You two are merely alpha males. I am an alpha female."

Knowing my men as I do, I spent the afternoon setting up the Rocky Road room to my specifications. I approved whole-heartedly of Devon's choices of female companions for this evening's pleasures. The stunning petite redhead who engaged in my first visit to the Bitterroot River Clan home, a tall raven-haired beauty with piercing blue eyes and a brunette sporting the sexiest pouty lips I ever saw joined me in my preparations. I informed them on the itinerary I planned.

I intended for this to go well. I wanted to develop a plan implementing a working relationship between the Bitterroot River Clan and the Salmon River Pride. While Devon's abode provided every means of sexual pleasure, we offered a safe haven for those who required it. Half our members wanted sex, a lotta sex. The other half, eh, not so much. Or not at all. Several needed time and a space to heal.

The four women just recently liberated from Scott's dungeon may require a more conservative atmosphere than the Bitterroot provided. I swallowed a sob as I wondered what kind of shape Tristan would be in when we found him. While investigating witches obtaining Were organs, I read

Scott's own handwritten notes detailing the horrors he inflicted upon the people he abducted. My cousin wasn't a Were, but I doubted that would stop Scott.

Mentally, I changed my train of thought. I needed to convince Malachi and Devon to form an alliance between the two clans. At our lodge, we ensured our members a calm, secure, safe environment where they remained comforted. Observing the women Scott abducted, I noticed a couple weren't responding well to the sexual nature of the Bitterroot River Clan home. Familiar with Rhiannon's recovery from her experience in Scott's laboratory, I knew some of the women needed more than Devon could offer.

I refuse to call them victims or even survivors. They didn't lose their identity and gain a new one as the terms implied. We provided safety and time while they healed. I considered them warriors because they endured more torture than any hero I knew. But I refused to change their identity or turn them into a statistic.

I re-focused on the task at hand. Utilizing two buff werewolves, we moved a couple easy chairs into the room, as well as a California king size bed. Between the easy chairs, I set a table, a bottle of Jim Beam and a bottle of Captain Morgan's along with a couple tumblers. In two corners of the room, I set up four-point restraints and blindfolds.

After dinner, I led the two alphas into the infamous Rocky Road room. The women awaited our arrival, reclined on the bed. "Take a seat, gentlemen." I pointed to the two easy chairs. Malachi raised an eyebrow, but noticing the scantily clad women, he acquiesced. Smiling. Devon nodded, taking his seat. Each poured their respective drinks.

"Gentlemen, for your viewing pleasure, let me introduce your women of the night." With a flick of my wrist, I changed into a sky blue lace teddy, high cut up to my hip bones. I turned to the women, showing the men my ass, revealed moreso by the thin string riding between my buttocks. I heard a moan from the easy chairs.

Turning towards the ladies, I smirked. "Our first lady is Natalie." Natalie climbed off the bed clothed in an emerald green baby doll dress. "Even though she's a tiny package, she knows how to offer pleasure to everyone. Her tongue is especially talented." While I described her, she walked the cat walk, twirling just enough, allowing a glimpse of her ass beneath the skirt of her dress, her long red hair flying around her.

"Next, we have Amelia, our candy girl." The long legged, brunette simpered in front of the men, in a pink silk negligee and high heels, sucking on a popsicle. She twirled around in front of the men, reaching down, straight legged, touching the ground. Underneath, she wore ruffled panties. She looked back at them, sliding the popsicle deep into her throat. Both men groaned. She climbed on the bed, feeding her popsicle to Natalie. Natalie swirled her tongue around the tip several times, before deep throating it.

"Our third lady, Celine, needs no description." The raven wore a strappy black leather corset and thong, with thigh high boots. Strutting before the alphas, she cracked a leather braided cat o' nine tails as she rocked back and forth, from leg to leg. She stopped in front of them.

"I am Shyenne. I love to fuck." I walked up to the two men. I laid my hands upon the table between the two of them, bending over, very low. My ass high in the air. As I bent over, my tits barely covered by my teddy, Celine spanked me with her cat o' nine tails. I gasped. Instantly, both men grew hard. She struck my ass again. I stood and walked over to the bed. Kneeling down, I laid across it, my ass in the air, legs spread far apart. Celine snapped her flog. Then, she draped the tips of the leather implement across my ass, swishing it back and forth. I moaned. She did this several times before striking me. I screamed. The men jumped. Drawing her implement of pleasure and pain back and forth between my thighs, she rubbed my clit, before lightly striking it. Natalie grasped my hands as Celine slid her popsicle between the folds of her vagina. She shivered as Celine touched her clit. Tangling my fingers through her hair, I pulled her head to me, thrusting my tongue into her mouth. Our lips dueled as our clits were assailed. Turning over, I ripped the teddy covering my breasts. Natalie moved down, encompassing one of my nipples in her mouth as I suckled the one thrust in mine.

The popsicle melted down to nothing and thusly tossed aside as Celine fell on her, her tongue worshipping her nether regions.

Amelia dragged her cat of nine tails back and forth over my cunt. As I suckled the tit in my mouth, she struck my clit. Once, twice, three times. I orgasmed. She dropped to her knees, drinking my juices as they flowed.

Both men jumped up to join us. We stood. Amelia and I led Malachi to one corner while Natalie and Celine drove Devon to the other. We restrained the alpha males. Starting at their feet, we each trailed kisses up their legs. Where the legs came together, we kissed each other. Then, licked the inner thighs, each one of us suckling a ball, running our tongues down the side of his cock. We French kissed one another, his rock hard shaft between us.

At some point we all ended up on the bed. The debauchery continued until only Devon, Malachi and I remained behind.

19

Something woke me. I "felt" around. Mictlantecuhtli, the Aztec God of the Underworld, stood at the end of the bed. I unintentionally aided in resurrecting the god when a witch kidnapped me while trying to rescue my Uncle Benito, Shaman for the Hopi tribe. The god crooked his finger at me, smiling provocatively. I 'ported from between Malachi and Devon, with an impish look on my face. He wrapped his arms around me, and we moved into astral space, re-appearing in a dense forest, but not my type of forest, a rain forest.

Raising an eyebrow, "Hi, Mictlantecuhtli. What's up?"

"I need your assistance in acquiring my spear. Xochiquetzal refuses to return it without a sacrifice," he explained, his arm lying across my shoulders.

"Whoa, buddy! I'm not dying for a spear!" I pushed against him escaping his arms, sinking into the earth.

He laughed, chasing after me. *Not that type of sacrifice. A sexual sacrifice, of sorts.* Mictlantecuhtli explained. *She's feeling rather neglected because she lacks the followers she had centuries before. Prior to returning the spear that rightfully belongs to me,* he stated in an aggrieved tone, *She requires a sexual sacrifice upon her altar where she will provide a blessing upon the maiden and my spear to me.*

I returned to rain forest. "What type of sexual sacrifice? The normal type of sex?" I questioned hesitantly, staying outside of his reach, ready to return to earth, if he made any sudden moves. "With who?"

"I don't understand the term "normal". Sex with me upon her altar in her temple," Mictlantecuhtli explained, smirking.

Don't get me wrong, sex with a god, I'm sure is a good thing for the most part. But the Aztecs tended to be rather bloody and violent when it came to sacrifices. And deadly. "Am I going to be injured, maimed, tortured or killed?"

He shook his head, laughing. "No. Xochiquetzal doesn't wish for women to suffer any injuries for worshipping her. Actually, she is quite probably the first goddess to elevate the standing of women. She believes the sexual experience needs to be fulfilling and enjoyable. For all involved."

"Well, I can't argue with that. Sounds like a goddess I'd worship." Being a Were, we openly engage in sexual exploits with others. Monogamy isn't a virtue we relish. And I admit Mictlantecuhtli isn't hard on the eyes. Jet black hair fell almost to his waist. His rock hard abs and well-muscled arms were the things wet dreams encompassed. He wore a short simple leather loin cloth. A chunk of obsidian hung around his neck and turquoise decorated his ear lobes. Around his right bicep, a bracelet of numerous colorful stones encircled the muscle. A perfect specimen of male yumminess. "Okay."

He took my hand and led me through the dense jungle, along a barely visible path. We walked across a fallen log over a roaring creek, ducking under low hanging trees. The trail disappeared as the foliage crowded around us. Branches scraped across my bare arms and pulled at my hair. The realization hit me I wore nothing.

Suddenly, the fauna parted, revealing a stone structure. A temple barely stood, crumbling walls covered by green vines. An assortment of colorful flowers entangled the vines and stones of the temple. Marigolds seemed to be the predominant flower. We entered through an archway. The interior weathered far better than the exterior. Aztec statues adorned the cobblestone walkway. Wreaths of flowers lay upon the statues, along with jewelry. A great throne embedded with gold, silver and gems faced the archway. To the side stood Xochiquetzal's altar, covered in assorted flower petals.

Mictlantecuhtli swung me up into his arms and carried me to the altar, gently laying me down. Surprisingly, it was softer than I imagined. Inches upon inches of petals covered the surface. The fragrance swirled around me as Mictlantecuhtli parted my legs, his tongue flicked my clit softly, over and over again. I moaned in ecstasy as he lifted my ass, burying his face deeper into me as his teeth caught my button. I orgasmed. Quickly, he lapped up my cum. As I rode the waves, he jumped up on the altar, straddling it. He pulled me onto his lap, forcing his large cock into me. I moaned as my slick tunnel slid down his shaft. Even though I had been sated earlier in the evening by Malachi and Devon, I hungered for what Mictlantecuhtli offered me. Eagerly, I rode him as he held my hips, allowing me to set the pace. He pulled my nipple into his mouth, alternating between biting me and sweetly suckling.

As I succumbed to my second orgasm, he slowed our rhythm and continued at a less frantic pace, easing me into a third. Once I finished, "I want you from behind, please." He flipped me around on to my hands and knees and penetrated me, even deeper. But he didn't let me take control, holding onto my hips, slowly he sank into me and pulled almost all the way out. A guttural moan escaped me as he tickled my g-spot. Wrapping one arm around my waist, he pulled me up against him, holding me tight as his other hand, grasped my face, turning my mouth to kiss me. Our tongues dueled, teasing one another as he maintained control, while he pumped into me, slowly increasing the pace. His hand dropped from my face to my cunt where he began to stroke and flick my nub. His other arm held me in check, not allowing me to alter our race to the finish. Finally, he acquiesced, pounding into me, lowering me down on the altar while he thrust deep inside me. The stone altar had no give and he sank deeper, harder into me than I'd ever known. He fisted a handful of my hair, pulling my face back to his as his tongue invaded my mouth. I swallowed his scream as he ejaculated into my center.

For many moments, his body laid on top of mine, heaving as he sought to catch his breath. Consciousness eluded me as I fought to catch mine. At some point, he climbed off of me. Then, gentle hands turned me over, onto my back, trailing from my cheek, along my neck, circling each breast and nipple, dripping down my navel, and flowing to my vagina. The soft fingers stroked my nub and slid along my labia and into my vagina.

A sweet mouth tasting of flowers kissed me as the fingers worked at my clit. Kisses trailed down my neck and suckled each nipple while the fingers stroked and teased. I reached a weak hand up, tangling in waves of thick black hair, the scent of marigolds swirling around us. As she reached my womb, she trailed soft kisses and whispered words against my skin. Before the meaning of her words registered, her head sank to my clit. Her tongue encircled, teasing my nub, her breath whispering against me as she lined my labia to my vagina and back again, and again, and again. I sunk down into the sensations of her tongue, her gentle fingers, the aroma of flowers, the soft altar I lay on. This orgasm felt so different than anything I'd ever experienced before. Typically, I want a harsh, hard, fast pounding as I fall over the waterfall.

Instead, butterflies kissed my entire body while enveloped in flower petals as she tickled my g-spot and clit at the same time. Almost like I was encased in warmth, feathers, the orgasm burst forth in a shower of snowflakes, raining down, lost in a blizzard, but entirely safe and warm.

I don't know how long I lay there before I awoke to the squawking of unfamiliar birds. Looking around, I lay on the stone altar, marigolds covered me. Mictlantecuhtli and Xochiquetzal were nowhere to be found. Torches illuminated the temple with some natural light pouring in through the archway. I sat up and swung my legs to the side of the altar. Surprisingly, my body didn't ache like it should have after all the sex I enjoyed in the last day. I walked out of the temple and sank into the earth, 'porting to the Bitterroot River Clan home and into Devon's bedroom, sliding back in between the two alphas.

"Mmmm. You smell awesome, like flowers." Malachi stated, kissing me.

"Marigolds." Devon corrected, turning my head to kiss me.

Malachi snarled, entering my vagina, pulling me on top of him. Not to be outdone, Devon grabbed a squeeze bottle of lube, pushed my legs far apart, poured it on my ass and buried his cock, balls deep. I moaned in ecstasy as the two men fucked me, trying to outdo the other. As one entered, the other withdrew, at a furious pace, pounding into me. Somewhere along the way, they traded places. All I knew was I had more orgasms in twelve hours than I ever experienced in my life.

20

Tristan spent the rest of the evening and the next day perusing the magic books in Eleanor's altar room, researching any and all spells that might possibly break the barrier. They tried a number of spells, including creating a dirt golem, opening a portal, speaking with the dead, shrinking, growing, polymorphing, and just short of calling a demon, the two prisoners held no luck escaping their jail.

Tristan admitted defeat.

The next option, the only option he believed available to them ... stealing Richard's magic from Scott and assimilate it into himself. Tristan didn't need to hit him with a sleeping spell. He failed to wake. Infection ravaged his wounds. Whether it be hours or a couple days, Scott's life had a finite expiration date. The healing spells Tristan cast appeared to keep him alive, barely. After killing Eleanor, J-Dawg refused to use his newly acquired skills to do anything that may improve Scummy Ball Sack's life in the slightest.

The food situation proved just as dire. Flour, water, honey, mustard and horseradish were the only items left. Tristan picked dandelions out of the yard, making a salad. He used pine needles for tea, but drew the line at eating bugs or worms. For now. He even used spell components from the altar room to make a soup, of sorts. He hated the idea of killing squirrels or birds, but realized the option remained.

After a hardy lunch, not, he returned to Scott's magic center, surveying the situation. Scott's magic appeared to be failing. The flame at the center barely glowed. The tendrils stood limp, hardly weaving about. Richard's magic looked worse. A weak pinpoint of light winked in and out. The tendrils lay weak, barely moving. The magic was dying.

Tristan picked up a tendril, feeding energy into it. The strand hungrily slurped it up. Another strand strained to reach towards him. He fed it. Placing his hand in the waning center, Tristan pushed magic, fueling it, pouring all he had into it. The center flamed, like oxygen blowing on fire. He realized he was out of time. If he didn't transfer the magic, like now, the magic would die. Scott would die. He would die. J-Dawg, well, he could eat grasshoppers and watch Nickelodeon.

After a good night's sleep, Tristan's magic regenerated. He needed to be as strong as possible to perform the transfer. Entering astral space, Tristan eased into Scott's mind. Moving past the areas he believed held Scott's psychopathology, he reached the magic center. Richard's magic lay beside Scott's, gleaming dimmer than before he infused it. Tristan studied it intently, noting it appeared to lay next to Scott's magic, but didn't seem embedded or assimilated. Cautiously, Tristan reached out and touched the surface. A wave rippled across the individual tendrils. He lifted it up, not as easily as Eleanor's but it offered little resistance.

Tristan carried it back to astral space and to his magical center. He placed it adjacent to his healthy vines. His individual strands eagerly reached out to the new ones, then recoiled suddenly, moving away. *Uh oh. That's not good.* Stepping back, Tristan observed the magic strains, trying to identify the issue. *Richard's magic is fire. Mine is earth and water. Did I try to attach fire to water? That probably wouldn't work. I need to attach earth and fire.* He picked up the dimly lit flame and placed it on the other side of his magic. *What spells would be similar among earth and fire?*

Mentally scratching his head, he considered what magic might overlap. *When does earth catch on fire? Lava!* He'd never created lava before. How would he start? Pull it up from the earth. Studying his tendrils, he searched for one emanating heat, then brought it forward. He moved Richard's magic closer to it. The weak strands reached for the one providing heat, eagerly sucking nutrients from it. Using strong earth strands from the base, Tristan wrapped them around, strengthening the foundation of the fire. The strands instantly revolted if water and fire came into contact.

This is kinda like transplanting flowers. I need to make sure I have a strong base with lots of nutrients available to feed both magics. The water and fire must remain at opposite ends with earth in the middle. Braiding the weaker strands with the earth strands strengthened the fire magic. The inner core began to brighten as more and more tendrils connected, integrated, assimilated, providing nourishment to the starved magic.

A tickling sensation occurred deep in his psyche. The fire magic rooted itself, attracted by the nutrients, empowered by the connections. *Scott must not have had any clue how to integrate his father's magic into his. Not that I do either. Having the knowledge of psionics and transplanting flowers seems to be in my favor.* Tristan entangled more and more strands, each one providing more strength and nutrition, building a stronger foundation. He spent a significant amount of time making connections. Focusing on the bases, he thought the foundations of magic would hold similar concepts.

Finally, not seeing any other strands to connect, Tristan surveyed his magic center. While two obvious factions of magic existed, common bonds united them into one. The once dying fire magic now flamed red, with blue spots growing in the middle. Tendrils sank down into his psyche, soaking up the nutrients. Tristan instituted all his ideas on how to fully incorporate Richard's magic into his own.

Tristan landed back in the living room. Scott slept? Comatose? On the couch. J-Dawg lay on the back, a long line of drool hanging from his mouth, almost touching Scott's forehead.

"Really? Torturing the unconscious dude?" Tristan asked, shaking his head.

Surprised by his return, J-Dawg jumped, the spittle dropping across Scott's face. "Oops. Sorry, not sorry." Flapping his wings, J-Dawg rose into the air. "Did ya get the transfer done? How do you feel? Let's blow this joint!"

"Okay, here goes nothin'!" Tristan attempted to teleport into astral space but he met the barrier. He returned to the living room. "Let's go outside and I'll try to dispel the ward." The two headed outdoors. Tristan walked to the edge. He cast the spell. The ward shimmered but held. "Help me out. Boost me. That seemed like it almost did it!"

"Alrighty!" The little dragon responded eagerly. "How do I do that?" J-Dawg asked. Tristan stared at him. The tiny dragon raised his paws up as he shrugged. "What? I never learned how. Scummy Ball Sack killed Eleanor before she taught me."

Tristan sighed. "Okay. I know how to boost. I'll teach you. I'm not sure how I do it, I've always just … did it." Contemplating the process, Tristan dropped onto the ground, sitting cross-legged. J-Dawg plopped down next to him, copying his position. A smile curved across Tristan's lips. "Okay, hold your paw out. Pool magic into your palm. Now, send a strand of it to me."

A string snaked its way to Tristan's hand. "Perfect. I'll cast the dispel and use your magic to boost it." As the spell hit the barrier, Tristan directed J-Dawg's magic to feed into it. Waves rippled across the ward as it shimmered, weakening. Where the spell made contact, a small hole opened. Tristan felt a tingle run through him, breaking his concentration, dropping the spell as the barrier bounced back into place.

"Damn ham butt, banana eared turkeys!" J-Dawg cussed, jumping up and kicking the ground. "What happened?"

Tristan laughed, tears gathering in his eyes. "Shay found me."

21

The sun called to me just before it broke the tree line. As awareness drifted over me, I found myself cuddled between two hot bodies. Without opening my eyes, I tried to remember who the bodies belonged to. To no avail. So, I sniffed. Oh fuck. Malachi. Devon. I did what any smart, successful, independent woman would do. I 'ported the fuck out, landing at my lodge, on the bank of the Salmon River. I took a moment. I took another moment. I took a third moment. Focus. Tristan. Tears filled my eyes. Angrily, I brushed them away. Opening a portal to my closet, I pulled out a pair of jeans and a sweatshirt.

What would Tristan do?

He'd try to 'port. He'd sink into the earth. When we 'port our molecules separate and mingle with the earth. I need Tristan's molecules. Our altar at Uncle Alberto's house. Immediately, I sank into the earth and reappeared in our sacred spot.

Zeke did a strange screech and attempted some sort of martial arts karate chop towards me, before he realized it was me. He tried to pull back his kick-punch and I blocked it.

"Sorry, Shy! I didn't mean it!"

I chuckled. "It's okay, sweetie. I appeared out of nowhere without any warning. You have every reason to be defensive. Good reactions!" I ruffled his hair. His mom slept near the altar in a sleeping bag.

"Any sign of him yet?"

I shook my head. "I'm going out on a limb. I'm gonna try to track his molecules through the earth."

"You're so cool. Can I watch?"

Half laughing, half sobbing, I inclined my head. I walked over to Tristan's spot at the altar. "Remnants of his molecules should remain in the soil?"

"Are you asking me? 'Cuz I totally agree with whatever you think. You're too cool for school. If you think so, I agree." Zeke vigorously nodded his head.

Again, I laughed. Right now, Zeke was exactly what I needed to boost my mood, attitude, confidence. "Okay, so I'm gonna meld into his place and suck up his residue, then search through the earth for it. I'm praying to every god who ever existed that I can locate his molecules through whatever ward is imprisoning him."

Zeke exhaled, "That is sooooooo cool!"

I almost busted a gut, laughing, tears rolling down my face. I wasn't sure if I was laughing or crying, but I nodded. After I gained control over myself, I sank into Tristan's spot at the altar.

We each had our own place. Growing up, the altar ended up being one of our team building magical exercises. I had located the old growth cedar tree up in the Selway Wilderness. I convinced, bribed, threatened, cajoled my siblings and cousins into helping me 'port the tree home. It took all of us working together to move the large slab. Uncle Alberto was very displeased when we appeared in his back yard with this incredibly large chunk o' tree. I convinced him that we needed to design an altar and develop consecrated ground to perform our family / coven rituals. We placed the slab across two large stones. Then, re-directed part of the Selway River to run under the rocks, carrying the energy of the water. It fed up one stone, through the slab, down the other, creating a magical circuit, binding earth and water magic, both elements our family gained power from. Each of us had our own spot at the altar that "spoke" to us, individually. So, by default, parts of Tristan's essence, molecules, pieces should remain in his spot?

I had no idea. But I hoped beyond hope enough of him remained here that I could trace other pieces of him in the place he tried to 'port from. Okay, it was a total complete absolute long shot. But it was all I had. I ran out of ideas. Tristan wasn't the strongest, most powerful of us. But he was our glue, our kickstand, the one we all counted on, no recriminations, no judgements, total acceptance.

I sank into the dirt, opening myself entirely to... earth, dirt, worms, decay, essence. I felt a tiny bit of Tristan and grasped onto it. Then another and another and another. I pulled his essence all together. And coalesced it. I wrapped myself around the feel of Tristan. I let his essence draw me in. Then I reached for more. I was pulled to my house, to 3D Investigations, to the Bitterroot River Clan house, and then I radiated out further. Several more stops led me to different locales but I didn't "feel" him. I hit more Taco Bells than I thought existed. His trail grew colder.

The realization hit me. "Scott travelled through astral space, not dirt. I need to see if I can track his molecules through astral space!"

"Sounds legit to me!" Zeke agreed amicably, as he followed me to each stop.

We 'ported to the Bitterroot River Clan home. I returned to the spot Tristan disappeared from. Sucking up all the Tristan molecules I could, I entered astral space with Zeke. I closed my eyes, focusing on Tristan's molecules. Blindly, I followed the bread crumbs of molecules left behind. Molecules proved incredibly difficult to trace through essence, as essence was molecules. I returned to the clan home. I tried to "gather" Scott's molecules. With a combination of the two, perhaps it may be easier to follow their path.

Just as I started to enter the astral plane, Shay 'pathed me.

"Hey, I came up with a way-"

"I found him! Come home, now!"

I grabbed Zeke and 'ported to Shay's location. She sat on the ground next to the Snake river and a pine tree.

"I performed a locate spell! For just a moment, I touched him! I left a trail to the location. Follow it!" Shay ordered, excitedly as she held onto the trail. I picked up the path, and, accompanied by Zeke, traced it through the earth. Then, I came to a boundary. A ward. A wall. Shay's trail led into the blocked area. I popped up as close as I could get. Zeke appeared next to me. We stood nosed up to a barrier.

Stepping back, I surveyed the scene. "We're in Oregon." Zeke informed me, checking the GPS on his phone. We stood within a forest of Ponderosa Pines. They grow quicker in Oregon but not as strong as in Montana. A small yard encircled a smaller cabin. Tristan sat on the earth, a tiny purple dragon, sat beside him. A tiny purple dragon? An impenetrable force field surrounded the area. I moved to the nearest tree and tried to port through, to no avail. I sank into the earth. I entered astral space. I screamed, yelled, pounded and basically threw a tizzy fit, to no avail. I couldn't get through. "Fuck!"

Tristan walked over to the barrier. He said something, but I couldn't quite make out his words.

"We need one of those cans on a string," Zeke offered.

I rolled my eyes. Tristan laughed, understanding the eye roll.

"I'll go grab a glass!" Zeke jumped into astral space and disappeared.

I leaned my forehead against the barrier, placing my hand on it. Tristan placed his with mine.

Zeke popped back with a glass. "Here! Try this!" I shot him an unbelieving look. "Seriously. Try it."

Rolling my eyes once again, I placed the glass adjacent to the barrier.

"This barrier fucking sucks!" Tristan stated in a tinny, hollow voice. Well, I could hear him.

"What have you tried so far?" I asked. Tristan shook his head, then held up a finger. The purple mini dragon flew into the house and quickly returned with a glass. High tech at work. I repeated my question.

"Uh, gee, dispel, detect magic, enlarge, shrink, light balls, snow globe barrier, talking with the dead, boosting a dispel, create golem, polymorph, create portal, abracadabra, hocus pocus, open sesame, and amuck, amuck amuck!" Tristan counted off on his fingers.

"Amuck, amuck, amuck? That didn't work?" I questioned, sardonically. "Where's Scott?"

"Scummy Ball Sack is comatose on the couch. I can't perform a healing spell strong enough to heal him. J-Dawg refuses to." Tristan explained, hooking a thumb towards the little dragon.

"I don't blame J-Dawg a bit. I'm assuming he's the purple dragon?" I asked. We both glanced towards him. Zeke and J-Dawg were performing magical machinations for each other in between throwing weird finger movements, probably trying to imitate gang signs. We both rolled our eyes.

"We almost broke the barrier when I dispelled it with J-Dawg boosting me. That was when Shay located me." Tristan explained.

"Okay, great. Yo, Zeke! Take a break from magical gangbangin' and come boost me," I informed him.

"Totally cool!" Zeke came running over to me, instantly forming a ball of magic in his hand.

I readied the dispel, then Zeke boosted me. I sent the spell to the barrier. Waves rippled from the impact zone. The barrier shimmered, shimmered, shimmered. Oh, fuck.

"Did the barrier absorb the spell?" Tristan asked softly, dejection flowing through his voice.

"Yup."

"What does that mean?" Zeke asked. Neither one of us answered. "Guys, what does this mean?"

"It means that if the spell doesn't take down the god damn mother fucking son of a bitchin' barrier, it adds magic to it," I explained, angrily. Who the hell created this damn barrier?

"Oh, that sucks." Zeke described succinctly.

"Yup." I replied. "Call reinforcements."

"And tell them to bring Taco Bell and beer!" Tristan added through the glass.

"And crickets!" J-Dawg chimed in.

Within a few minutes, the cavalry arrived, sporting Taco Bell, beer and crickets. Shay showed up empty handed while Lance brought beer, Nate grabbed tacos and Bane sported crickets, with Jadan laughing.

"So, what are the crickets for?" Bane inquired, elbowing his brother in the gut.

"J-Dawg! The little purple dragon!" Zeke waved to him inside the ward.

"Why haven't you let Tristan out yet?" Lance inquired, readying a spell.

"No!" Shy and Zeke shouted. Tristan and J-Dawg waved their arms from inside.

"The barrier converts the spell to power, reinforcing the ward!" I stated hurriedly.

"We found out the hard way," Zeke informed them, describing the earlier events.

"Oh, shit. It sounds like you almost brought it down." Lance commented.

Tristan piped up in a tinny voice. "J-Dawg and I opened it just enough for Shay's locate spell to tag me. We need to be ready to dive through when it opens. Wait 'til I grab Scummy Ball Sack." Tristan turned quickly, jogging back to the house. In a matter of moments, he returned, with Scott slung over his shoulder. "J-Dawg, stay right with me. Be ready to fly through once it opens."

"Lance, cast the spell. Everyone one else, boost him," Shay announced, as they all readied their magic.

As Lance prepared the spell, everyone else connected and funneled magic to Shay. She tethered to Lance and he cast the dispel. Again, shock waves rippled across the barrier. A pea sized hole appeared and began to grow. The barrier changed to a light peach incandescent color. The hole reached the size of a dinner plate. The color deepened to sweet pink as the hole grew to a beach ball. The dome began to shimmer.

Zeke grabbed the Taco Bell bag and threw it inside, then the beer and crickets became airborne, as the shimmer overtook the waves. The hole began shrinking. Tristan dropped Scott, like a sack of potatoes, cussing. J-Dawg peeled a scale from his hide and threw it in the hole, allowing a small hole to remain open in the barrier. The barrier enveloped and absorbed the magic. Everyone stood quietly, on both sides of the barrier, for several moments.

"Good thinking, Zeke." Shay stated softly, finally speaking.

"Tell your brothers I'm adopting you. You just became my favorite person!" Tristan dove on the Taco Bell bag, digging out a taco. He inhaled three before he stopped for breath. He rolled his eyes in ecstasy. "You ordered grasshoppers? Dude, there's tons of grasshoppers in here! Why didn't you order caviar? Or something else?"

"These are crickets. Kinda like the filet mignon of steak. I don't like fish eggs!" J-Dawg shuttered as he let lose the bugs. Hopping after them, he popped crickets in his mouth as he caught them.

"What are you doing, J-Dawg?" Tristan asked bewildered, as he drained a beer, watching the little purple dragon jump after the crickets he just freed.

"Dinner tastes so much better after you hunt it!"

A chorus of chuckles crossed through the ward.

"How's Scott?" Shay asked, studying him through the dome.

"Comatose. I've healed him with spells as much as I could. His magic failed to regenerate. He attempted to cast a healing charm and he tried to steal magic from me, so I clocked him." Tristan cracked another beer. "Scott knew he was dying. He knew we were out of food. And still, he chose to keep us trapped." Tristan shook his head.

"How long has he been unconscious?" Bane asked, leaning against the barrier.

"Two days."

"We can't let him die." Shay stated, exasperated.

Bane and I looked at one another. Neither one of us planned to heal him.

"Call his mom. She likes him. She'll heal him," Tristan suggested. "Maybe she can convince him to trigger the ward, allowing our escape from this hell hole."

The idea held merit. "I'll go talk with her and bring her back," I offered, sinking into the earth. I popped up at her front yard, and leapt up the stairs, then rang the doorbell. Mary answered within a few moments.

"Shyenne! What brings you here?" Mary asked, drying her hands on a towel. "Did you find them? Is Scott alright? Tristan?"

At the mention of my name, Kayla appeared by her side.

"The good news is we found them. The bad news, we can't get through the ward. Scott has been unconscious for two days. Tristan dropped the ward long enough to allow Shay to tag him the first time, and we sent food through the second time." I inhaled, "Tristan thought you might heal Scott and convince him to drop the barrier."

"You transported food in but they couldn't escape?" Kayla asked, bewildered.

"Our combined magic created a very small hole. Then the ward absorbed the magic, intensifying the barrier." I explained further. "Tristan and J-Dawg cast the initial dispel allowing Shay to tag him. The rest of us cast the second and almost brought the barrier down, but failed when it assimilated the power."

"J-Dawg?" Kayla questioned.

"Please. Let's go to the barrier. You can heal Scott and try to convince him to dispel the ward," I tried to hasten them along. "We can answer all your questions once we free them."

Mary nodded, stepping out of the home with Kayla at her heels. We 'ported to the barrier.

Upon our arrival, Lance, Bane, Jadan and Nate clued Tristan in on the events leading up to today. Mary and Kayla ran towards the iridescent wall, seeing Scott lying on the ground on the other side. An ashen hue, he looked very near death. Green goo oozed through the bandage on his abdomen. His left arm sported a burnt stump at the wrist. Mary cried out as Kayla smacked a hand against the barrier.

Kayla started to cast as we all screamed, "No!". She froze, turning her gaze to us.

"Your magic will only reinforce it! We need Scott to lower the ward. Mary, you're the only one that can convince him to dispel it. They've been out of food for two days. Scott needs medical attention." I explained further, "J-Dawg, the little purple dragon threw one of his scales into the opening before it re-sealed. There's a small opening we're using to communicate. I think you could cast through there to heal Scott."

Tristan looked up from inhaling a burrito, "I've been doing what I can to heal him, but I don't have much for healing spells. We ran out of hydrogen peroxide and gauze the same time we ran out of food."

Focusing on the small opening, Mary chanted in a foreign language, sending a healing spell to Scott. It coalesced around his body, soaking into his abdomen. As she continued, twinkling lights circled, dipping and swirling around the wound. After a minute, she dropped to her knees, weakly. Bane caught her, lowering her gently to the ground.

Scott stirred, moaning. Whimpering. He opened his eyes and looked around. "Tristan!"

"Yo, Dude. Suck it up. Your mom and sister are here," Tristan stated. "Wanna taco?"

"Water."

"How 'bout beer?" Tristan offered, handing him a bottle.

"Yes! Help me up! Why are we outside?" Scott glanced around as Tristan offered him a hand.

"We hoped they could bring the barrier down. They didn't but Zeke threw food through the hole before it closed. And J-Dawg placed one of his scales to keep the hole open at least a little ways. The damn ward sucks up magic cast against it, further empowering it."

Scott looked around, noticing the members of the Nez Perce Coven, Nate, Zeke, Kayla and his mom. "Mom! Finish healing me!"

"Release the barricade. I need to lay hands on you. Your wounds appear grave and your system is seriously depleted," Mary said, shaking her head. She leaned against he barrier. Tears rolled down her cheek as she looked at her oldest child.

Guzzling the beer, rivulets ran from the corner of his mouth. He finished it off quickly, then turned his attention to the on-lookers. He weighed his options. "Heal me as much as you can from there." He countered.

Mary whipped her head back, surprised. "Scott, you're seriously injured. You need to be healed. You probably need to be treated in a hospital!"

He scoffed. "As soon as the barrier comes down, that bitch will hand me over to the cops. I'm lookin' at the death penalty or at the very least, life in prison."

"So, what's your plan, Einstein?" Jadan asked, slamming a fist against the dome. "Sit in there and starve to death?"

"Heal up and 'port out!"

"What about me?" Tristan asked, nonchalantly, sipping a beer.

Shrugging his shoulders, "Cannon fodder, insurance, slave, toy," Scott responded, glancing at him, then returning his gaze to his mother.

"You are such a Scummy Ball Sack! You don't deserve to breathe!" J-Dawg alighted on Tristan's shoulder.

"What the hell is that thing? Is it a tiny dragon? A fairy dragon!" Scott sounded incredulous. He formed a fireball into his palm. "Give it to me!"

"I don't know what alternate universe you inhabit, but I'd become a yellow headed, five legged purple octopus before I'd ever choose to be your familiar, you evil maggot infested rat!" J-Dawg succinctly described.

"Unless your witch is dead." Scott threw the fireball. Tristan countered with a water ball, extinguishing the fire. With a well-aimed throw, Tristan sent a second water ball his direction, aiming at his abdominal wound. He hit his mark. Scott dropped to the ground, doubled over in pain. J-Dawg created an orb around him.

"You fucking prick! Let me out of here!" Scott screamed. He tried to 'port, but remained stuck. He pounded on the orb. "You mother fucker!" He attempted several different spells but it appeared his magic ran out.

"Scott! Calm down! You don't know that you'll be convicted! I'll hire you the best lawyers! There's no proof you did anything wrong!" Mary sniffled. "You're a good boy." She added, softer, doubting her own words.

Bane and Jadan looked at her like she was senile. I swallowed down a mouthy retort.

"I don't stand a chance, Mom. Between the Were found in my basement and the four I imprisoned in the Bitterroot, there's all the testimony needed to fry me." Scott remarked, blithely.

"Don't forget about your handwritten documentation of the Weres you tortured and killed along with your father and fiancé," I reminded him. "Mindy already confessed to everything."

Scott rolled his eyes, "She is so full of shit. Like I would ever marry her."

Yeah, that was what he focused on. I thought to myself.

Kayla looked between Scott, her mother, the rest of us and Tristan. "And you kidnapped Tristan. As an act of good will, you need to free him. Scott, you fucked up. You fucked up bad. Now, you have to do something to earn a little good will. To show you aren't a murderous psychopath. Demonstrate you have empathy, compassion. Tristan cared for you. After you kidnapped him. Free him." Kayla implored.

Scott looked into his sister's eyes, "Nope."

Everyone remained quiet for several moments. Mentally, I inventoried our assets. Let's see. We're all drained of magic. Except Kayla. Tristan and J-Dawg used up their magic. The hole in the barrier. Dokwl could fit through the hole. I called my little Kachina familiar. He appeared behind me, scampering up my back, burrowing into my hair.

"What are you going to do, Scott? Your mom healed you somewhat. But your infection will return. You need way more healing. Looks like you won't be 'porting through the little dragon's orb any time soon. Sounds like J-Dawg is hardly your biggest fan." Jadan asked, leaning nonchalantly against the barrier. "Observing your stomach, looks like Tristan re-opened the injury." He nodded towards the blood and gunk seeping through the filthy bandage.

"We won't be sending any medical supplies through." I glanced to

Mary. "I'm sorry. We won't allow you or Kayla to heal him or transfer magic, anymore. We acted in good faith. J-Dawg, if you don't mind, keep him imprisoned in your orb. We'll figure out ways to keep Tristan and J-Dawg fed. But not you."

As evilly as a little purple dragon can laugh, J-Dawg did, rubbing his paws together, gleefully. "The only thing that would please me more would be chocolate covered crickets! Have fun shitting in the orb, Scummy Ball Sack."

"I like him," Jadan nodded approvingly towards the hovering dragon.

"Me, too." Bane agreed.

Scott looked towards his mother, imploring. "Mama, I need help. You don't know what they'll do to me."

She gazed at him, eyes filling with tears. "You just told all of us what you intend to do to Tristan. The man who helped save your sister. Who took care of you while you held him hostage. I don't know what they'll do to you, but it won't be worse than what you intended to do to Tristan or have done to others." Mary turned to me, crying, "I'm going home now. Call me the next time you want to attempt to bring the barrier down." Her voice broke. "I'll help."

Jadan wrapped an arm around her and 'ported her back home.

"Kayla, I did this for you. All of this was to heal you. To save your life," Scott implored.

"How did four women locked in dungeons in your basement in Montana benefit me?" Kayla inquired, not seeing a connection.

The mother fucker possessed the gall to laugh. "That was my reward for a job well done. If we hadn't come up with the spell to heal you, you'd be dead."

"Mom came up with the idea to use Were essence. Tell me. Did you ever even try it?" Kayla inquired, her voice held no emotion. By the look on Scott's face, obviously they hadn't. "Or were all of you enjoying kidnapping, torturing and killing the women?"

"In this world, ya gotta find joy where ya can, lil sis." He stated, with

134

a laugh.

Normally, Bane tends to be the most patient, controlled, level headed of all of us. He flipped. He ran full tilt towards the barrier, sword raised.

As he smacked it, J-Dawg squealed. "Holy ectoplasmic elk shit!", letting loose a light bolt impacting the same spot.

Dokwl screeched, throwing ice crystals into the impact site. I pulled *Eadala,* as a crack appeared. Lance 'ported out. Performing his signature move, the windmill, Bane repeatedly struck the barrier. Staying out of his way, I moved to the side and stabbed into the cracked area. Jadan jumped to Bane's opposite side, jabbing his sword into the fracture. He wedged it in, twisting, turning, leveraging up and down. Shards fell out. Tristan grabbed a chunk of firewood and beat it from the interior. J-Dawg threw bolt after bolt. The crack spider webbed. Lance returned, sporting a five-gallon jug of water. Shay pulled the water out of the jug, encircling the opened fissure, freezing it in the cracks. Her and Lance sent water through all the cracks, freezing it, forcing the cracks to grow. The ice reached out, holding the edges back, intruding on the open fissures, refusing to allow the barrier to reform. Jadan, Bane and I spread out, continuing to beat on the wall, creating more cracks. Bane jumped to the top, stabbing down into it. Nate, Zeke, Dylan, Kayla and Lance 'ported out and returned with more five gallon jugs. Lance landed next to Bane, pushing water into the cracks, and instantly freezing it, splitting the ward. Bane punched through, then with sweeping motions, continued breaking it up. Lance filled the open space with ice.

Kayla followed Jadan, filling in the growing opening with ice while Zeke and Dylan moved with me, forming ice along the openings I generated. Once the three locations joined to one large iced area, everyone halted. Bending over, gasping for air, falling to our knees, Bane, Jadan and I quit.

Scott laughed. "What the fuck are you going to do now? If you take away the ice, the barrier reforms. It's still inaccessible."

Bane, Jadan, Lance, Shay and I 'ported through the ice, entering the ward. Tristan grabbed J-Dawg, 'porting them outside.

"Dumb fuck. Nez Perce Coven is water and earth elements. We 'port through water. Ice is water." Jadan stated simply. "Now, what were you saying, about Were women being your reward for being a rapist psychopath?" Bane and Jadan stalked around the orb incarcerating Scott.

"Boys, boys, boys. He will suffer miserably in prison. He's a spiny ass weakling. Without magic, he'll be everyone's girlfriend. Then he'll start to learn what it felt like for all his victims. First hand." Shaylenne explained.

Bane backed off. Jadan snarled gutturally. Scott cringed back within the orb. Jadan laughed. "What a brave little psychopath."

"Who knew all we needed to do was piss Bane off to break the barrier?" Tristan muttered, shaking his head.

"So, what now?" Bane asked, rolling his eyes.

Everyone hesitated. "I vote we wait him out. His infection will kick back in, he'll be comatose, drained of magic. It'll be the safest way to move him." I suggested. We all turned to Kayla, knowing she would be the most likely to object. She inhaled a deep, shaky breath, then nodded, her eyes filled with tears.

"I vote that I suck all the air out of the orb, wait 'til he's unconscious, then put some air back in 'til he revives, then suck it back out. Do that about ten, twenty times. Scummy Ball Sack deserves to suffer," J-Dawg spat.

"If you ever get bored hangin' with Tristan, you're always welcome at my house. You're awesome!" Jadan exclaimed, shaking his head and laughing at the little dragon.

J-Dawg flew over and landed on Tristan's shoulder, encircling his tail around his neck. "Sorry, 'cuz, J-Dawg and I are best buds. We bonded over Scummy Ball Sack." Tristan replied, smiling as the two performed a fist bump.

"Well, a few of us should go-" Shay started just as Al ported in, next to Tristan.

"Hey, Dad! Long time no see. Did ya bring Taco Bell?"

Al enveloped him in a bear hug.

22

Barking noises erupted from Zeke. "Oh, that's my dad! Hey Dad! What's up?" Steve 'ported to the site within moments. Lance explained the mechanics of barrier to them. Then, Shay recounted the arrival of Mary and Kayla. I added our epic battle against the barrier.

"When we tried to dispel the barrier, it created a small opening, but not big enough to fit through. Zeke threw food and beer to Tristan before it closed. J-Dawg slipped a scale to keep a small hole available for communication," I added.

"J-Dawg?" Stephen inquired.

The tiny purple dragon waved at him from his perch on Tristan's shoulder.

"You never located the origination of the ward?" Al asked.

Tristan shook his head. "We searched bottom to top of the house, with no luck. The barrier appears to be password protected. Scummy Ball Sack knows the password. J-Dawg served as Eleanor's familiar but doesn't know what it is."

"Scummy Ball Sack killed Eleanor!" J-Dawg hollered out from the safety of Tristan's shoulder.

"How the hell do you know that?" Scott asked from his prison, bewildered.

"I saw you!"

"Scummy Ball Sack is Scott," Zeke explained to his dad, chuckling.

"Is there a particular reason why you all are inside the barrier?" Steve questioned.

"Scott didn't understand the importance of ice. We demonstrated it for him." Bane answered, leaning casually against Scott's prison.

"It was a teaching moment," Tristan added, nodding.

"So, what's your plan?" Steve asked, glancing around at all of us.

"We're going to camp out here, maintain the ice barricade until Scummy Ball Sack lapses back into a coma. Then, we'll turn him over to the Nez Perce County Sheriff's Department. It's the safest way to ensure his return to jail." I described.

Al and Steve contemplated the plan. After many moments, and not coming up with a better alternative, they both nodded.

It took two days. We provided Scott with water and minimal food. From Taco Bell, of course. After building camp, outside the barrier, we explored Eleanor's home. J-Dawg refused to reveal Eleanor's magic room to the rest of us. I decided to search for the ward. Meanwhile, Tristan went home to shower, change clothes and make another Taco Bell run.

I walked into the kitchen, gazing around in second sight but saw nothing. Pointing to the ceiling, "Is there anything up there?"

Hastily, J-Dawg responded, "We searched the attic, too." Shaking his head, "Nothing up there of interest. Nope, nothing at all!"

Yeah, that wasn't obvious or anything, I rolled my eyes. "You're a horrible liar. What about the roof?"

He cocked his head to the side. "We didn't search the roof."

I had my starting point. "I'm going to 'port to the roof and have a look-see. Holler if you need me." Entering astral space, I travelled to the top of the house and appeared next to a weather vane made of wrought iron with a lightning rod attached. Gently, I materialized and crouched down. Looking at the ornate design, I realized it was a magic symbol. I didn't recognize it. Using second sight, I saw the magic attached to it. The ward. I attempted to dispel it. Nothing. Physically, I tried to pull it off. It zapped me.

This might prove more difficult that I thought. I sat down cross legged on the wooden shingles, staring at the offending item. I didn't recognize the type of magic used to cast the ward. Whoever performed the spell and created the ward surpassed me magically. I formed an ice ball and hit it. It broke into chunks, not harming the vane in the slightest.

I studied how the spell weaved into the weather vane. The sun empowered it but I didn't understand the mechanics behind it. Far different than what I was familiar with. What if I pulled the iron out of the weather vane? Like the bars holding the women in Scott's cages. I wasn't affecting the spell, just the container for it. Connecting to the vane, I gently tugged on the iron. Initially, nothing happened. When formed, the process produced a pretty sturdy piece. Using more force, I pulled harder. I felt the bonds beginning to give a little and continued to apply pressure. Finally, a chunk emerged, followed by more. Once enough of the vane fell to pieces, the spell dissipated, with nothing to mold it.

Triumphantly, I landed next to Scott's orb. Flashing him an evil smile, I assessed his condition. His abdominal wound seeped. He failed to respond to my antagonizing. Looking into his eyes, I saw consciousness, but no acknowledgement of my existence. It wouldn't be too much longer.

The first night, we settled around in our sleeping bags. Except Kayla. She returned home. I guess she couldn't stomach watching her brother deteriorate before her eyes.

"Hey! Wanna see my new trick?" Tristan asked. He set a bunch of pine needles, pine cones and twigs in the center of a fire ring. In his hand, he formed a flame. He tossed it towards the waiting site. It turned to water, then evaporated into steam. "Damn! Wait! Let me try it again." A fireball shaped in his hand. Again, he threw it towards the ring. Again, it turned to water, steam, evaporation. "Dammit!" He conjured a flame, then knelt down, setting it to light the needles.

Everyone cheered.

"How the hell did you pick up the ability to create flame?" Lance asked, as he clapped his approval.

"I may have liberated Richard's magic from Scott." Tristan acknowledged.

"I'm a strong proponent for stealing magic from undeserving ball sacks." I replied, placing a marshmallow on a stick to roast over the flames.

"He stole Eleanor's magic, before he killed her. I transferred hers to J-Dawg. They both practice light magic." Tristan explained as he stuck a marshmallow on a stick. "I hoped that J-Dawg would know how to control the barrier if he possessed Eleanor's magic. When that didn't work, I thought that with Richard's magic, mine, J-Dawg's and Eleanor's we might be able to get through the ward." Tristan bowed his head, after his confession.

Shay responded first. "Tristan, you held out longer than any of us would. Not only did you feed, provide medical care, you offered comfort to the dickwad holding you captive. I guarantee you Bane, Jadan and Shy would have killed him the first chance they had." We nodded in agreement. "Lance would have stolen all three magics as soon as he fell asleep." Lance hesitated, considered the idea, then, nodded.

"The first day we ran out of food, I'd have taken his and Richard's. You don't need to feel guilty, sorry or remorseful. You're a better person than all of us. Combined."

"I voted we kill Scummy Ball Sack the first day. I voted we steal all the magic and leave him a brain-dead zombie like he did Eleanor. I wanted to barf on his wounds." J-Dawg stated filled us in on his opinion.

Everyone around the fire cracked up, laughing at the cute mini purple dragon. He giggled. Dragons giggle??? How does one learn more about a dragon? Ask questions.

"How did you come to be here, J-Dawg?" Lance asked him, as he meticulously built a s'more.

"Eleanor hatched me. Scummy Ball Sack killed her. He brought Tristan. Tristan and I worked together to overthrow the evilness of Scummy Ball Sack and steal the magic he stole from Eleanor and the magic from his dad to free us."

"Huh. Wow." Lance pondered the information for a moment. "We should check out the integration of magics in the two of you." Lance stated.

"Tomorrow. We've eaten way too many s'mores, drank a whole lotta rum and suffered too much drama today. Tristan needs to relax and enjoy life a little before we invade his brain," I announced, as I passed a bottle to Bane.

Tristan nodded in agreement.

23

The next morning, Dylan headed to 3D Investigations, Nate and Zeke decided to check on their mom, Jadan went to see about things at his clan home. Bane 'ported to Seattle to ensure everything ran well within the Pacific Region. Tristan watched while Shay, Lance and I entered astral space to inspect his handiwork in transferring Eleanor's magic to J-Dawg. Scott remained in the bubble, semi-conscious, semi-alert, semi-oriented.

We ooh'ed and aaah'ed over the little dragon's magical center. Never seeing light magic before, the glowing intensity surprised us. A bright star glittered at the center. Individual strands weaved around, comprised of sparkles. It appeared larger than typical, asymmetrical with one side seeming smaller than the other. Only one nucleus remained. The two magics appeared to assimilate into one naturally.

We returned to our bodies at the camp site. "What did you think?" Tristan asked, warily.

"Very well done. The two magics combined. You can barely ascertain there was more than one body." I complimented him.

"With time, Eleanor's magic will be fully incorporated into J-Dawg's," Lance observed.

Tristan appeared surprised. "Awesome! Did it seem to be rooted strongly into his psyche?"

Shay nodded, "Yeah, it's almost completely assimilated into his own magic. There's no way to differentiate between the two. They combined to the point where only one center remains."

"Cool! Let's go check mine." Tristan turned to the little dragon, "J-Dawg, would you mind keeping watch?" Turning back to us, Tristan explained, "I want to show you how I performed the transfer and the issues I dealt with regarding incorporating fire with water and earth."

J-Dawg snapped a salute, "You can count on me, Boss!" He cast a light bolt and began marching the perimeter of the camp.

Lance laughed outright, while Shay and I stifled ours. Tristan rolled his eyes, "Thanks, Dude. Let's go."

The four of us entered astral space, then Tristan's mind, towards the center of his magic.

J-Dawg patrolled camp for about ten minutes before Al showed up.

"Halt! Who goes there?" J-Dawg inquired swinging his light bolt around towards Al.

Al raised an eyebrow. "I'm Tristan's father. What are they up to now?" He asked, noting the four meditating forms.

"They're checking out how well Tristan transferred some of Scummy Ball Sack's magic," J-Dawg replied, still pointing his light bolt at Al.

"They're what?! I need to go check on them!" Frustration flowed through Al's voice as J-Dawg created an iridescent sphere around the four.

"Sorry, I'm supposed to keep them safe. No one disturbs Tristan while he's mucking around in someone's brain. Especially his!" J-Dawg resumed his patrol, light bolt in hand.

"Look, J-Dawg, I need to help Tristan. He can't transfer the magic on his own. He doesn't know what he's doing!" Al implored the little dragon.

"Yes, he does. He transferred Eleanor's magic that Scummy Ball Sack had stolen to me and I'm doing just fine," J-Dawg proclaimed, haughtily.

Complete surprise kept Al at a loss as to what to say. Stephen arrived within a few moments, quickly taking note of the dragon walking a beat while Al stared at him agape, "What's up?"

"Tristan, Shy, Shay and Lance are evaluating Tristan's transfer of some of Scummy Ball Sack's magic. He appointed me as captain of the guard. Al's freaking out that Tristan transferred magic to me and to himself." J-Dawg explained. Stephen stared at him wide eyed.

"Uh, it's perfectly fine for Al to assist Tristan. In fact, Al is considered a master at psionic magic," Stephen advocated for Al.

"What's psionics?"

"Psionics is the art of fixing one's mind by using mental magic," Steve explained.

"Huh. Tristan said his dad would be interested in Scummy Ball Sack's psycho-ology."

"I think that's psychology," Steve corrected, swallowing a chuckle.

"No, it's psycho-ology. The reason why he's a psychopath. Parts of his brain don't talk to other parts of his brain, according to Tristan." The little dragon expounded to the two coven leaders.

"J-Dawg, I'm Tristan's father. It's alright for me to check on him," Al tried another tactic.

"Yeah, well my dad is a Lambana, well-known tricksters. So, sayin' you're his dad, doesn't install any confidence in your motives. Once Tristan tells me you're safe, then I'll believe it." The tiny dragon resumed his patrol.

Stephen attempted to hide his smirk while Al looked completely bewildered. He pulled out his phone. "Hey, we need your assistance here at camp. Have your brother stay with your mom, but 'port out here."

Within moments, Zeke landed beside his father. "What's up?"

Stephen stated, "Apparently, Tristan stole Scott's magic to break out of here. They're all checking on the procedure. J-Dawg is protecting Tristan and won't let us near him."

Zeke walked over to J-Dawg, "Hey, dude! What's aapp?" They performed a complicated hand shake ritual culminating in a burst of lights raining down.

Rocking his head back and forth, J-Dawg replied, "Your dad summed it up accurately."

"Is he dangerous?" Al asked Zeke.

Zeke laughed. "Do you really want to find out?" He pointed a thumb at J-Dawg. "He's a dragon. He's protecting Tristan. For right now, he's okay."

"I need to check on them!" Al argued emphatically.

"I'll run grab Taco Bell. Maybe if we hold a taco under Tristan's nose, he'll come back!" Zeke suggested.

Al rolled his eyes, while Stephen tried not to laugh. Zeke popped out. "I thought I had it bad with three sons. With the six kids you dealt with, it's any wonder you retained any sanity!" Steve commented. Al just shook his head.

Zeke returned in about ten minutes. "One great thing about looking for Tristan, I know where all the Taco Bells are in the Northwest! J-Dawg, hold a taco under Tristan's nose. He'll come back."

J-Dawg hesitated, then nodded. He reached a paw - arm- clawed appendage- through the orb and took the proffered taco. Holding it under Tristan's nose, for a few seconds, he turned his back. Al quickly moved towards the protected area. He reached a hand towards the orb and was thrown back, landing next to Zeke.

"Holy shit! I guess the little dragon does pack a punch!" Zeke announced, stifling a laugh at the expense of a coven leader.

24

"You stole his magic?" Al questioned, searching Tristan's eyes for any negative signs.

Shrugging his shoulders, "I took Richard's magic. We ran out of food. I couldn't find the ward. I wasn't sure if the ward would drop if he died." Tristan met his father's eyes. "By talking with J-Dawg, I surmised Eleanor cast the ward, not him. He killed her and it didn't disable the barrier."

He took a deep breath, "I honestly worried I'd starve before anyone found me. Since he'd been unconscious, I studied his magic, at length. He didn't integrate Eleanor or his father's magic into his own. Both of them laid next to his magic center, very close to dying out, I might add. Since they weren't integrated, they received very little nourishment, compounded by his body stealing all energies to heal his wounds. Eleanor's magic suffered the most, going the longest without proper nutrients. In all actuality, transferring the magic proved fairly easy to accomplish. I think so, anyways. J-Dawg seems fine and Eleanor's magic recuperated and is flourishing within J-Dawg."

The dragon nodded in agreement and flexed his arm muscles. "I'm stronger than ever. That protective orb? Yeah, I got that from Eleanor's magic! Cool, huh?"

"Totally cool! That was awesome how it made Al FLY backwards ten feet!" Zeke agreed, high fiving J-Dawg as he came to hover by him. "So, dude, what kinda dragon are you?"

"I'm a light dragon. My magic involves manipulation of light and what you see," J-Dawg explained, creating dancing lights swirling around Zeke.

"Are you, like, an illusionist?" Zeke questioned as he gazed in wonder at the twinkling spots.

"Yep, I am!"

"Who the hell name's a dragon J-Dawg?" Al muttered under his voice.

"My actual name is," J-Dawg emitted this horrific sound similar to a humpback whale, alligator growling and a robin chirping simultaneously. My ears almost bled. The glass shattered in the windows of the cottage. "J-Dawg seems easier for humans to pronounce than my actual name. Do you want me to say it again, enunciate it clearer?"

A chorus of "No's" met his suggestion. Zeke and J-Dawg laughed. "Dude! That was awesome!"

"I want to check you out, see what you did to yourself," Al remarked, shooting a dark look at J-Dawg. "Tell your dragon, I'm allowed."

Lance and I stifled our chuckles as we prepared to go with Al. Considered a master of psionics, we looked forward to his observations.

The four of us entered astral space and then "traveled" to Tristan's mind. We found his magic area. I was familiar with his center. We studied each other's throughout our childhood. A new development occurred. Whereas his magic used to emanate an earthy substance with water flowing energy running through it, now, an area of flames lay on the outer edge with the earth magic creating a barrier against the water, separating the two.

Carefully, I approached the area, intently studying the assimilation between all the magics. In places, it appeared he braided the earth and fire together. Tendrils reached, mixed, tangled. The "roots" burrowed into the magic center creating a firm foundation. The center of the fire magic flamed a bright yellow color. Strands on the outer edge glimmered a light yellow with spots of gray.

Al knelt beside me, studying the strains. *Strands nearer the earth magic appear healthier than these further away. The gray indicates severe malnourishment of the magic.*

I observed the movement of the individual strings. *The ones closest to the earth strands appear stronger, waving around energetically. The outer tendrils seem weaker.*

We studied the integration of the fire to Tristan's magic center. While it was clearly separate, the strands interwove between the two, creating numerous entanglements. Individual strains burrowed into Tristan's psyche, rooting in and under the primary magic center. I couldn't see a safe way to retract the flames without disrupting or harming Tristan.

Al reached a hand to the flames. *How did you transfer the magic?*

It wasn't embedded in Scott's psyche. I literally picked it up and moved it here, through the astral plane. Tristan explained.

Gingerly, Al tried to lift the section. It didn't budge.

We returned to the yard from astral space.

"You did a really good job of integrating the fire into earth magic. There's no separating them. It appears fully integrated into your own." I observed. "I don't think I could have done a better job. Why is the water not bound to the fire?"

"What happens when water and fire meet? They destroy each other. When I initially began combining them, the water recoiled from the flames and vice versa." Tristan explained.

Lance and Al nodded, contemplating his observation and agreed he did a good job. Tristan jumped in the air and did a fist pump. "Awesome!"

"Well, Clark's magic will need to be returned to his family," Stephen stated, grimacing.

I laughed. "That's not happening. Like Al said, the magic is assimilated into Tristan's. It can't be removed, without causing serious, irreparable damage to Tristan and his magic. Scummy Ball Sack should have considered that before he kidnapped Tristan and locked him in a cabin with no fucking food! The loss of his father's magic falls solely on him. Tristan felt that this was the only way he could escape." I took a defensive stance in front of my cousin.

"Let's discuss this at a later date. Right now, we need to transfer Scott to law enforcement control and make arrangements for medical care." Uncle Al stated. Everyone turned and looked towards me, to heal him.

I shook my head. "I don't waste magic on psychopathic rapists. It'll be a cold day in hell before I heal him." No one else offered up. No one else possessed the healing skills his injuries required. Other than Bane. And he was in Seattle. "Call his mother and have her meet us either at the hospital or the sheriff's department. She can heal him. I vote for the sheriff's department."

My sister and cousins nodded in agreement. Sighing, "Actually, we should 'port him to a hospital for stabilization until we find someone willing to heal him. His injuries are substantial." Uncle Al overruled me. I rolled my eyes. Sympathy wasn't high on my list.

I noticed J-Dawg sat glumly on a step of the cottage, watching the proceedings. Tristan noticed, too, and moved to his side. "Yo, dude! What's up?"

Turning a plum color, he tried to adopt a tough dragon facade, "Aw, your leaving."

"Hell, yeah! Aren't you coming with us? I'll take you to our house. You'll love it there! We have two rivers, mountains, caves, trees, very few people. It's totally cool!" Tristan described, enticing him to go with him.

J-Dawg glowed a neon purple and flew into Tristan's arms, wrapping his claws around his neck, hugging him. Then, remembering himself, he back pedaled and replied in a deep voice, "That's cool, dude!" Everyone hid their smiles.

While Steve, Al and I escorted Scott to the hospital, Tristan, Shay, Lance and begrudgingly, J-Dawg, relocated all Eleanor's magic items to our home, to peruse at a later date.

25

Dylan met Al, Steve, and I at St. Joseph's Hospital in Lewiston, as we 'ported a comatose Scummy Ball Sack. Dylan called Detective Swanson to inform him of our whereabouts and our prisoner. Steve called Mary. I stood over Scott, ensuring he didn't wake up or go anywhere.

"He's under a sleep spell and is unresponsive due to his injuries and infection," I informed the ER nurse as she began obtaining his vitals.

"Is there a reason for that? What happened to him?" She glanced at me before poking a needle into his hand for an IV.

"The short version is he escaped from jail. He's wanted in connection with the rape, torture and murder of numerous female Weres. Due to his magical abilities, he poses a significant risk for escaping and injuring others. He attacked my cousin, friend and me. I defended us." I briefly explained as Swanson walked into the room.

"He's under arrest and isn't to go anywhere without my express permission," Swanson ordered as he walked into the room. Catching sight of Scott, he exclaimed, "Holy shit! What happened to him?" Swanson turned to me.

"We went to liberate the four women he held in his basement. He threw a fireball at us, I defended us." I provided the short version.

He surveyed me, skeptically. "You look no worse for wear."

I harrumphed. "You should have seen Lance and Nate Kane. They suffered severe burns, requiring immediate healing. Scott 'ported away, kidnapped my cousin, Tristan, and held him hostage for over a week before we

150

finally found them. Tristan hadn't eaten in several days. Scummy Ball Sack refused to allow Tristan to leave or tell him how to get passed the wards."

"Scummy Ball Sack?"

"An eloquent nickname he earned."

Swanson huffed.

The door burst open as Mary and Kayla rushed into the room. Mary sobbed as she looked at her son, "Why haven't you healed him?" She asked me, tears running down her face.

"I won't heal him."

"He needs to be healed immediately! The sleep spell should be dispelled. He's in custody now." Kayla declared hotly.

Detective Swanson interjected. "Scott broke out of jail and has been charged with the kidnap, torture and murder of five women. Montana has charges of kidnap, rape and torture of four more women pending. He can be healed and stabilized, but I want him left unconscious."

Mary sank into a chair next to his hospital bed and began performing several healing spells. Kayla surveyed the scene and then turned towards me, fire in her eyes and forming in her hand. "Where is my father's magic?"

Splaying my hands to my sides, "I don't have it. Let's talk somewhere else. Your brother doesn't have the wherewithall to get caught in another magical battle at this time. I think we're perfectly capable of discussing this situation without resorting to violence. Steve Kane and my uncle are here somewhere. As our Coven leaders, they can mediate this discussion." I offered, trying to keep the peace. I really didn't want to defend myself against Kayla. Or start an inter coven war.

She looked to her brother and nodded. We entered the hallway and she whirled on me. "Where is my father's magic?"

I reached out for Al. *Kayla demands her father's magic be returned. She's holding a fireball.*

On my way. Uncle Al responded, sighing.

"Kayla, you know Scott kidnapped Tristan and held him hostage. Tristan couldn't 'port past the ward. They ran out of food. Scott refused to let Tristan go, explain how to get through the ward or allow him to contact anyone for help. Tristan went four days with very little to no food. As a last ditch effort to save his own life, he psionically transferred your father's magic and assimilated it into his own. He incorporated it very well, weaving it into his magic. It would be extremely dangerous to try to separate your father's magic from Tristan's."

"Well, you damn well better figure it out! He is not keeping my father's magic." Kayla stated angrily. "I demand our family magic be returned."

"Given the circumstances, you have no right to make any demands. Your family manipulated my wife into performing the spells to transfer the magic. Numerous laws were violated getting the crystals into the jail. Scott used the magic and crystals to escape. He's wanted in numerous states for kidnapping and murdering Weres. Montana will be charging him for the four Weres recently rescued from another of his dungeons." Steve lined out succinctly. "You aided in the search for Tristan. You know he was shielded behind incredibly strong wards. Shyenne located him a day after he finished integrating the magic. Alberto inspected the transformation. There isn't a safe way to de-assimilate the magic."

"Scott wouldn't be alive if not for Tristan caring for him. Tristan cast numerous healing spells, cleaned his wounds and provided much comfort and care to Scott," Uncle Al added vehemently.

Mary walked out into the hallway. "Shyenne, I can't dispel your sleep spell. I've healed all I can. He's stabilized." Detective Swanson followed her out of the room.

"Mom! Tristan stole father's magic from Scott! They refuse to return it!" Kayla implored her mother, tears welling up in her eyes.

"My main concern at this time is stabilizing Scott and waking him up. I want to ensure his health. Right now, his legal situation is far more concerning than Richard's magic." Mary inhaled a sob.

Swanson stepped out of the emergency room door. I looked to the detective. "Do you want me to wake him up? My recommendation is to leave him asleep until he's safely ensconced behind magically protected bars."

"Oh, really! I don't think that's necessary! He has significant injuries and needs medical care!" Mary responded. "His magic is weak!"

Swanson shook his head, "Leave him out until he's transferred. I don't want to risk losing him again. We've spent four months looking for him with at least four new victims."

"Five. He killed a witch named Eleanor in Oregon. He hid Tristan in her home," I updated him.

"We'll need to inform the local PD about that." Swanson sighed, running a hand through his graying hair.

"He may have cognitive deficits related to the magic transfer. He needs to be awakened now!" Mary insisted, as tears ran down her cheeks.

"Cognitively, he appeared fine when we checked him at the cottage," I argued. "Well, other than the psychopathology. That was clearly evident. You saw him, spoke to him. His mental capacity hadn't changed with the loss of his father's magic."

"I'm sorry Mrs. Clark. Scott poses too much of a danger to society. Until he is secured, he'll remain under the sleep spell." Detective Swanson stated in no uncertain terms. "I'll make arrangements for his transfer immediately."

26

"You in a good mood or a bad mood?" Al asked.

Sighing heavily into my cell, "What now?" I asked, standing up and walking out the French doors at my lodge. I walked to the river bank, watching the Snake river flow by.

"Kayla petitioned the Governing Board of Covens regarding the return of Richard's magic. Tristan and I need to appear before them, tomorrow. I want you to testify to Scott's actions since you performed both investigations," Al remarked. His voice sounded cool, unattached. But I knew he must have been terrified for Tristan.

I thought highly unpleasant thoughts towards Kayla. "Alright." I sighed, again. "What is the Orchard Coven's position on Kayla's demand?"

"Steve told her he won't support her claim at the risk of Tristan's health and if she continues to make the demand, she'll be excommunicated from the Coven." Al replied.

A small glimmer of relief grew within my stomach. "What is the Governing Board of Covens? I've never heard of it before," I questioned as I assimilated the information.

"The Board is elected by all witches to decide disagreements between witches and covens or between covens. They'll hear both sides and make a determination."

We sat in a large conference room at Lewis-Clark Magic School. At the front of the room sat five witches behind a mahogany table. I didn't know any of them. After learning of this hearing, I researched the group more. The members were elected from a pool of candidates nominated by other witches. Every witch voted for their top five choices. Requirements of the positions included being a witch in good standing and level four or higher. I noted types of magic practiced didn't matter.

There were no seats available in the conference room. In fact, many stood at the back of the room. Al and Tristan sat at a table facing the Board. Kayla sat at a table adjacent to them. Just like a courtroom. Dylan, Lance, Shay and I sat behind my uncle and cousin. Bane, Jadan, Malachi and Devon sat in the second row, behind us. Numerous large screen televisions lined every wall with more witches watching.

A witch about my age threw crackly lights up in the air, quieting the room. She wore a green suede short dress and brown heeled boots. I identified her as an air witch, level three. "The Governing Board of Covens calls to order this meeting. Alistair Montague, Headmaster of Lewis-Clark Magic School, level five, Druid." A very tall, thin man stood up and bowed. He wore thick glasses, a tweed suit with a bow tie.

"Penelope Walters, Walters Coven, Coven Leader, level five, water." A dowdy, middle-aged woman stood up and bowed. She flashed a sweet smile.

"Magna Humphry, Chair Person, Palouse Coven, Coven Leader, level five, earth." The third person at the table stood, reddish-brown hair pulled back from her face tightly. I could tell she sized up all of us.

"Morgan Rosewood, Tri-Cities Coven, level four, water." I guessed her age to be mid-thirties, very pretty and knew it. I recognized her name. She was a celebrity of sorts in the magical world. She made quite a name for herself in Magic School and studied in Scotland where it was rumored she had found the Loch Ness monster.

"Isaiah Smithton-Black, Walla-Walla Coven, Level five, Elemental." This guy gave me the creepy crawlies. I checked his aura. It was not good. Darkness, waves, deep purple, browns, navy, black. He turned to me and our eyes locked, briefly. He realized I saw his aura.

"State your name and affiliation," Magna, the chairwoman of the Governing Board of Covens directed.

"I am Kayla Clark, member of the Orchards Coven, level four, fire magic."

"State your claim."

"Tristan Mendoza of the Nez Perce Coven stole my father's magic from my brother and refuses to return it to our family. My father willingly transferred the magic to my brother. My brother didn't agree to the transfer from himself to Tristan. The Nez Perce Coven refuses to return the magic, claiming it will cause irreparable harm to him. He is a thief and the magic belongs to the Clark family."

I laughed outright, standing up and walking to the center of the council. "Are you going to fill in the rest of the blanks or shall I?"

I heard Lance whisper, "Oh, fuck."

Kayla inhaled sharply. But said nothing.

Alrighty, then. "I am Shyenne de la Angelino, member of the Nez Perce Coven, Earth and Water level four, classified as a catalyst. Richard Clark, Kayla's father, and Scott Clark, Kayla's brother, were arrested and incarcerated at the Nez Perce County Jail awaiting trial for numerous charges including kidnapping and murder of numerous Weres in the course of magical experimentation with Were bodily organs. A friend of Scott's impersonated their attorney and handed off two crystals to Richard. One to transfer his magic to Scott and one for Scott to teleport out of the jail.

"After Scott escaped, he killed a witch in Oregon and kidnapped, raped and tortured four Were women in Montana. When we attempted to liberate the women and take him into custody, he magically attacked myself, my cousin, Lance Mendoza and Nate Kane, causing severe injuries to the latter two. I defended us with a magical sword, cutting off his left arm and striking a wound to his abdomen. We retreated. I transported Lance and Nate to safety, with Scott pursuing us. When he saw we 'ported to the Bitterroot River Were Clan home, he immediately teleported away through astral space. I chased him to his parents' home."

I nodded towards Kayla, "Kayla and I located him in a secured family vault. He 'ported out, traveled to the Bitterroot River Were Clan Home and kidnapped Tristan." Again, I nodded towards Kayla, "Kayla assisted us for six days attempting to locate them. The ward Scott hid behind proved too strong for any of us in either coven to penetrate with any type of spells or scrying."

Tristan rose to his feet. "I am Tristan Mendoza, member of the Nez Perce Coven, level one, classified as the crime scene whisperer." Several chuckles rang through the room. A stern look from Alistair, Headmaster, quickly quieted them. "The ward proved too strong for me to 'port astrally or through the earth. In fact, I couldn't even locate the ward. For over a week, Scott held me captive. He refused to allow me to leave or provide me with the knowledge to pass through the barrier. Four days into my captivity, we ran out of food. All we had for sustenance was water, flour, mustard and horseradish. And a beehive with honey outside in a tree.

"I provided care for Scott, performing healing spells several times a day, as well as sleep spells to allow him some comfort from pain. Due to his injuries, his magic failed to regenerate. I provided meals with what little food we had. He realized our dire circumstances and his severe wounds. I implored him to allow me to contact his mother for help. I lacked the ability to offer proper treatment of his injuries. He wanted me to transfer power to him. I refused. Scott lacked the ability to heal himself, activate the healing rings he wore or create a healing charm."

"Why didn't you just let him die or kill him? It sounds like it would have been easy enough to do," the dowdy, sweet looking lady, Penelope questioned.

"I didn't believe he cast the ward and figured his death wouldn't affect it either way." Tristan shrugged. "I'm not a killer. My father raised me to help, not injure, provide comfort, ease pain. I realize he's a psychotic prick, but I like his mom and Kayla. I thought my family would find me quickly."

He sighed. "By day four, I realized I had to do something else. Scott appeared to be dying from his injuries. I was going to starve to death. As many of you may know, our coven has significant psionic abilities. Mine are about the weakest, but I grew up with Lance, Shy and Shay. What I lack in abilities, I make up for in knowledge. I understood the mechanics Shyenne used when she developed the ritual to heal Kayla. So, I spent the next two days investigating Scott's magical center and creating the process to transfer the magic. I figured my only hope was to gain enough magic to locate and remove the ward. The only way to gain more magic," he shrugged, "was to take Scott's. When I checked his out, I saw that even though he transferred the magic from Eleanor and his father, he hadn't actually incorporated it into his own. The magics weren't receiving nourishment. The connections were extremely minimal. Removing them from Scott proved simple."

"Who is Eleanor?" Magna questioned.

"She was the witch who owned the house we stayed in. She set up the ward. Scott stole her magic and killed her." Tristan explained. "Implementing Richard's magic into me took significant work due to the juxtaposition of water and fire. But I realized my only hope of escaping was to fully incorporate the magic into my own. I had to be able to-"

"Is there something wrapped around your neck?" Morgan broke in.

Tristan smiled impishly as the little purple dragon appeared, curled around his shoulders. "This is J-Dawg. He was Eleanor's familiar and witnessed Scott killing her. He, too, was trapped behind the ward. J-Dawg chose not to make himself visible to Scott. I transferred Eleanor's magic to him before I incorporated Richard's, hoping that he might use Eleanor's magic to open the ward. But it didn't work. When I transferred the magic, it fully integrated, but J-Dawg didn't receive the knowledge or ability to remove the ward. That was day five. I realized I had no choice but to transfer Richard's magic into my own."

"So, you received a dragon and my father's magic?" Kayla replied haughtily.

"My intention wasn't to steal your father's magic. My intention was to live and not die by starvation," Tristan stated.

"Alberto, you're an expert in psionics. Is it possible to remove the Clark magic from Tristan?" Alistair questioned.

"Prior to answering, identify yourself, please," Morgan smiled deferentially to my uncle.

"Alberto Mendoza, Coven Leader of the Nez Perce Coven, level five, water and earth, classified as a mentalist," my uncle responded, nodding in acquiescence. "It is not. Tristan performed an admirable job of incorporating the fire magic into his earth magic. I don't know how familiar the council is with psionic magic."

"I am in need of education." Morgan smiled beguilingly at Uncle Al.

"Tristan discovered water and fire magics are incompatible. He found he could incorporate earth and fire. Your magic center is made up of individual strands. Each strand denotes a particular skill or spell. The tendrils combine, entangle and coalesce as your magical skills grow. He located individual vines similar in nature within the different elements." Al explained. Many of the council members looked at him blankly.

"Like, a lava ball in earth magic is similar to a fireball in fire magic. That was the first connection I successfully made," Tristan explained. The members nodded in understanding at Tristan's explanation.

"The individual strands make up a whole, and like a plant, roots grow down, seeking nourishment. In the magic center, the roots seep into the psyche which provides the appropriate amino acids and nutrients to fuel the magic. If the magic is rooted into the psyche, then removing it is extremely difficult, requiring psionic surgery which will more than likely cause severe neurological damage to the patient. Scott has no neurological damage related to the removal of Richard and Eleanor's magics."

"What neurological damage does he have?" Mary questioned from her seat behind Kayla.

"The damage which was already present related to his sociopathology. Of note, Richard suffered severe neurological damage related to the removal of his magic which has left him in a vegetative state. Scott retains his intelligence, verbal skills and exhibits the same level of rationale he possessed prior to the removal of the magics." Al explained.

"What are you basing that on?" Kayla questioned.

"I compared the video interviews relating to his arrest regarding the kidnappings and murders of Weres pertaining to the acquisition of a pituitary gland for you, and his current state now. There has been no meaningful change, whereas your father once was a highly intelligent man with significant verbal and rational thinking skills. Now, he's a vegetable."

"Scott failed to incorporate the magics into his magic center, making it easy for Tristan to harvest them. Tristan, however, worked very hard to incorporate the magics into his own, believing it to be his only means of escape. Lance, Shyenne and I evaluated the integration. We found no way to remove the Clark magic without causing severe harm to Tristan, and disrupting his own magic."

"Perhaps, Tristan should have thought about that before stealing my father's magic!" Kayla exclaimed.

I rounded on her. "Perhaps Scott should have thought about that before he kidnapped Tristan! And held him against his will for six days!" It took all my self-control not to punch her. But I held myself in check. I'd already created mayhem within the Were hierarchy. Should probably try to not create upheaval in the Governing Board of Covens.

"Ladies! Both of you hold your tongues, or I'll remove them. Tristan, would you agree to examination by a witch of our choosing?" Magna inquired.

Nodding, "Of course, as long as my father is present."

"Magna, who would you recommend?" Penelope asked, turning to look at her.

"Does anyone have any recommendations?" Magna asked the gallery.

Several members replied, "Al."

Magna huffed and clarified, "Anyone other than a member of the Nez Perce Coven?"

No one responded.

After several moments, Morgan stated. "I have some minor psionic abilities. My grandmother performed healing psionically. I understand the theories behind it. If we take a field trip and Alberto explains the integration process, perhaps we can determine for ourselves whether or not the magic can be safely removed." Morgan proposed to Magna.

"From an educational standpoint, I'd like to accompany you as well," Alistair interjected. "What is the Orchards' Coven's response to Kayla's claim?" Alistair questioned Steve Kane.

Steve Kane stood up. "I am Steve Kane, Orchards' Coven, Coven Leader level five, Wiccan. We believe Kayla is completely out of line. Scott acted extremely dishonorably, in fact, criminally. He may be facing the death penalty in two different states. His actions alone dictate he forfeit all his magic. Richard chose to transfer his magic to Scott with the knowledge of his previous actions and knowing Scott would use it to escape from jail and the pending charges. Richard voluntarily relinquished his magic. He has no standing regarding ownership of his magic. If Kayla continues with this ridiculous stance, she, too, will be excommunicated from the Orchards' Coven. I have discussed this with her and she is aware of our position."

Kayla lifted her chin, blinking back tears. But standing strong.

"Mary, what is your stance on this?" Alistair questioned Mary, in a softer tone.

Sighing, she stood up. "Our family was once as high as a family can reach. Now," tears rolled down her cheek, "We've lost everything. My husband is incarcerated and in a vegetative state. Scott will not see the light of day again. Many people, mostly women, were severely victimized and even killed. We owe amends to many. We need to change the face of the Clark family." She stifled a sob. "The Nez Perce Coven, Shyenne, gave you your life, Kayla. We owe them. I hate to imagine what Scott would have done to Tristan…" A sob broke forth. "Tristan can keep the magic. Perhaps, he'll use it better than our family has." She buried her face in a handkerchief, as she cried quietly.

Kayla roughly brushed tears off her face, at her mother's words. "I demand my father's magic be given to me," she stated in a quiet tone.

"I believe the Clark magic should be turned over to the Clarks. I don't think we want to start a precedence of stealing others magics because someone's afraid they may die," Penelope stated flatly.

"So, it's alright for someone to use that magic for the kidnapping, torture and rape of Weres?" I argued back.

Penelope laughed. "I don't care about Weres in the slightest. I don't have a problem with spell experimentation on them. At least the furry fools have some use."

I inhaled deeply. "What about the witch he killed? And the other two witches whose whereabouts are unaccounted for?"

"There's no proof he killed a witch and there's no proof Kiki and Rosie aren't alive," Kayla defended her brother.

"Actually, J-Dawg witnessed Scott stealing Eleanor's magic and killing her," Tristan remarked. "He tells everyone and anyone willing to listen about the incident."

"He can speak?" Alistair asked, surprised.

"Yes, I can talk," J-Dawg responded softly.

"Make your introduction, full name and affiliation, please," Magna requested.

I broke in, "Actually, ma'am, you don't want him to pronounce his full name. It'll break all the glass in the room, and perhaps in the buildings."

"Very well, then. What do we call you?"

"J-Dawg is my name. I've chosen to be Tristan's familiar. I'm a light dragon."

"What do you know about Scott Clark's involvement with Eleanor?" Magna asked the dragon.

"Eleanor brought him home from the farmer's market late last spring. She told him how to get in and out through the ward." Uncurling from his perch around Tristan's neck, he sat on his shoulder. "They were in the kitchen. He cast a spell on her, paralyzing her in place." J-Dawg swallowed a sob. "He cast another spell transferring her magic into a crystal. Then he incorporated her magic into his." A crystal tear rolled down his cheek.

Shaking his head, "She wasn't the same. She couldn't talk anymore. She walked around aimlessly, like she was looking for something. I tried to heal her, but it didn't help. Scummy Ball Sack would tell her to do things, like cook dinner, wash dishes. At first, she understood and did as he ordered. But, she deteriorated until she didn't understand what he wanted. She stopped walking." The crystals flowed freely down his face. Tristan caught them in his hand, scratching J-Dawg between the ears.

"She couldn't do anything anymore. He yelled at her, yelled in her face. Sometimes, he hit her. But she couldn't defend herself. I didn't have enough magic to protect her from him." More crystals flowed down. Softly, "Scummy Ball Sack strangled her. Then, he levitated her outside and lit her body on fire. He came back in and performed a clean-up spell where she had lain on the couch. He turned the television on and started watching music videos while her body burned outside. He'd throw more fireballs on her body until there wasn't anything left."

The room fell very quiet. I heard a crystal tear drop hit the wooden floor.

"For the record, Scummy Ball Sack refers to...?" Magna asked softly.

"Scott," several of us answered.

"That's the nomenclature J-Dawg uses to refer to Scott," Tristan explained further.

"And the two witches unaccounted for?" Morgan questioned.

Dylan stood up. "Dylan Delrikkio, member of Nez Perce Coven, not yet leveled or categorized, wholistic. I've performed numerous searches, along with the aid of Shaylene de la Angelino. Shay is equal to Shyenne level wise. Rosie is a level one, if anything. We haven't found any sign of her. Rosie worked for us at 3D Investigations. She didn't belong to a coven."

Stephen Kane stood up. "The Orchards' Coven tracked Rosie to the middle of a rocky mountain. She impersonated the attorney and transferred the crystals to Scott while he was in jail in Nez Perce County. Kiki, the second witch, is a member of the Orchards' Coven. We haven't found any sign of her. The Nez Perce Coven found both of their spell books on Scott's bedside table in his house in the Bitterroot Valley in Montana. The spell books are currently being held as evidence by law enforcement in Montana."

Morgan's head whipped back, as the other members of the council understood the importance of spell books. A witch wouldn't voluntarily part from her spell book. "Did you perform a search for her at the cottage and grounds once the ward was dropped?" Morgan asked.

We all looked at each other, then Tristan. "Don't look at me! I couldn't find myself, let alone anyone else." He scoffed.

"We will return to the site and perform a search," Al responded to her question.

"J-Dawg, did Scott ever show up with anyone else?" Magna asked him.

He shrugged his shoulders, "I never saw anyone other than Tristan. Usually, I hid when he came. He did come in late one night a few months after he killed Eleanor. He lit a big fire in the yard and kept it burning like when he disposed of Eleanor." Magna nodded her head.

"Why would he kidnap Tristan? It sounds like he typically chooses women," Isaiah remarked, confusion on his face as he tried to make sense of a psychotic's actions.

"One of his first victims was a homeless male Were he picked up. Scott's own detailed accounting of his crimes described torturous actions he perpetrated on him," I stated.

Shrugging, "Well, that was just a Were," Penelope commented. I ground my teeth, staring daggers at the bigoted bitch. Lance stroked my arm, trying to calm me.

Barely containing his anger, Al stated, "Tristan is a recognized witch. He is a member of a coven. He descends from a very strong witch family. He has more integrity and compassion than most witches I know. How many people in this room right now would have provided care for Scott under these circumstances?" Shay raised her hand, as did a few people in the audience. No one on the board signaled. I didn't raise my hand. Kayla looked around, noting the vast majority would have allowed him to die.

"Tristan accepts everyone. He tries to make us all happy. Whatever happens in the world, he sees the bright side. He makes me… optimistic. He makes me believe… that good is possible. That human nature is inherently good." Al's voice cracked.

I laid a hand on Al's arm, giving him time to recover his composure, "If Alistair and Morgan are ready, we can help prepare you to travel astrally into Tristan's magic center. Tristan will describe the process he used to integrate the magic and explain the condition of how he found Richard's magic within Scott."

"I want to go, too." Kayla spoke up.

I bit my tongue. Uncle Al tensed beside me.

Nodding, "That's fine. I think it would help Kayla understand the process if she observed my magic area," Tristan agreed, readily.

Inwardly, I groaned. The kid is too damn generous. "Sit back and relax. You need to enter into a meditative state, then move to the astral plane. Tristan and Al will guide you through the maze that is Tristan's mind."

Al and Tristan sat back down in their chairs, then entered astral space. I took up a defensive stance towards the audience. Lance came around the table and stood guard facing the board members. Bane and Jadan each stood at either end of the table.

Penelope and Margaret started conversing. "I think it's high time we passed a resolution allowing experimentation with Weres in magic."

Margaret nodded her head. "I agree. At least there would be a use for the furry creatures." She shuddered.

"The regeneration properties hold so much potential for healing spells. Organs from a Were could be options for transplants. I bet the chances of organ rejection would be greatly reduced." Penelope added.

"I've always wondered about a Were pelt. Could it –"

Jadan slapped a hand on the table, creating a loud bang. Half the people in the gallery jumped. "Bane! We have been so rude!"

"We've been rude?" Bane stressed the "We", as he turned to his brother.

Jadan laughed, a wide smile crossing his features. "We've forgotten our manners. We failed to introduce ourselves." Jadan stood up and strolled in front of the council. Isaiah raised a hand to his mouth, covering a smile. Margaret appeared annoyed at being interrupted. Penelope shot him a haughty look. "I am Jadan de la Angelino, member of Nez Perce Coven, level two, water and earth, classified as a fighter. And Heir Apparent to the Selway River Pride. This here," he pointed to Malachi, "Is Malachi Delrikkio, one of the D's in 3D Investigation, member of Nez Perce Coven, wholistic, level and category not yet set. 'Not yet set' means that he and his brother, Dylan, are really fucking powerful. Malachi is mated to Shyenne and is the Alpha Male of the Salmon River Pride."

I glanced at Penelope and Margaret. The color drained from their faces.

"Devon wave your hand." He waved. "Devon Ballantine is Heir Apparent to the Bitterroot River Were Clan. The four women Scummy Ball Sack kidnapped, tortured and raped belong to his clan. And last, but most certainly not least, Bane de la Angelino."

More Weres than us were in the room, as a chorus of 'Rah!' broke from each Were at our leader's name, Jadan being the loudest. Penelope looked like she might shit her dress.

"Bane de la Angelino, level two, earth and water, classified as the Warrior King!" Jadan growled, "Also, the Regional Alpha for the Northwest Were Clans, Prides, Packs, Herds, Flocks, any way any Were chooses to identify."

He laughed, shaking his head, "I'm so sorry, ma'am. Where are my manners? I cut you off. You were saying something." Jadan scratched his head. "Something about … pelts … Yes, Were pelts. What were you saying about Were pelts?"

Margaret and Penelope remained speechless.

Sighing, Jadan continued. "I'm so sorry to interrupt your train of thought. I guess you forgot what you were saying." Jadan turned his back on the women and returned to his post at the table, watching over Al and Nate. Isaiah openly laughed at the women. Honestly, I've never been prouder of my brother than that moment.

27

$\mathbf{T}$ristan met Kayla on the astral plane while his father collected Alistair and Morgan. Together, they moved into Tristan's mind. *You all are my witnesses that I do have a brain, when others accuse me of being a brainless twit.* Tristan commented as they flowed down the path.

Alberto indicated the different areas of the brain, pointing out the electrical charges sending messages to the throughout the sections. Alistair asked numerous questions. Al explained the relationships between brain function, psionics and the magic area. Finally, the tour group reached Tristan's magic center. In the middle, earth magic flourished as the tendrils wove about, excitedly. Next to it, the water magic flowed in waves, intertwined with earth. On the far side, flames licked wildly, mixing with the earth but veering away from the water.

When I initially moved Richard's fire magic over, the flames flickered dimly. The roots of the magic weren't embedded in Scott's psyche. To receive nourishment the roots need to be burrowed in. The center barely glowed. Due to Scott's physical condition, the magic was dying. I easily pulled out Richard's magic. Tristan bent over, grasping the fire magic. He tugged. While it strained, it stayed planted. *I noticed the individual strands slurped up energy from my hands and wove towards the earth magic. But I couldn't mix individual strands. They had to be of a similar nature.* Tristan held out a braided strand. *This is the first connection I made, the lava ball and the fire ball. If you look closely, you can see how they melded together, more than braided, blended. At the base, I realized I had to plant it into my psyche, but I was afraid to dig into my ... well, my brain. I studied how my earth magic gleaned on. I took these tendrils at the base of fire and intertwined them with the earth. I figured that the foundation of magic would be similar across all practices. That helped to provide nourishment to the starved strands. Even now, the magic looks so much healthier than when in Scott.*

Why wasn't my dad's magic integrated into Scott's magic? Shouldn't fire be attracted to fire? Kayla inquired as she knelt down, stroking the tendrils.

It's not as simple as just saying the words, doing the ritual, without forming some connections, ensuring appropriate nutrients feed the magic. Al explained.

According to J-Dawg, Scott used a spell with a crystal to transfer Eleanor's magic. In his mind, the two magics lay in close proximity to his magic, but wasn't touching, wasn't embedded. It was like a plant just being laid on top of the dirt, without digging a hole or packing dirt around it to ensure its assimilation. Tristan explained further. *I could easily pick up the whole chunk of magic, transport it to astral space and then transition it to my magic center. I realized I needed to ensure it was securely planted and receiving appropriate nutrition if I wanted it to work. I'm guessing that's why he didn't seem to have any extra magical abilities associated with Richard and Eleanor's magic.*

If you want to touch a tendril, it'll show you a magical skill. It's kinda cool. I touched one of Eleanor's strands. Totally over my head. I didn't understand any of it. Tristan explained.

They all reached out and stroked a flame. Exclamations of wonder surrounded Tristan. He gazed at Kayla. She knelt down, gently stroking different areas, surveying the integration of the magic. Abruptly, she gained her feet and stepped back. Morgan took her place, studying individual tendrils and the base of the magic, embedded in Tristan's psyche. She grasped it and pulled. But the fire magic didn't budge.

What the fuck? Are you trying to kill my son? Albert exclaimed, pushing her back. *You can't just try to uproot the magic! Specific steps must be adhered to!*

Alistair and Kayla looked at her in shock.

Can the magic be ... cut off at the base? Or would that be like removing the roots from a plant? Alistair questioned.

I'm not entirely certain, but I wouldn't recommend it. Al answered.

I believe it would destroy the magic. As you see, each strand holds an entire spell or skill. By cutting it at the base, you're cutting off part of the magic. You wouldn't have the complete spell in either place. I don't know if it will regenerate or not. Tristan pointed out.

The members of the field trip contemplated the information. With no more questions, they returned to astral space, then the meeting room.

"After reviewing the assimilation of the Clark magic by Tristan, I do not believe it can be removed without causing irreparable harm to Tristan or completely destroying the magic. In my opinion, Tristan should be allowed to keep the magic. Richard Clark voluntarily gave his magic to his son, Scott. Scott chose to rape, kidnap and murder others. He doesn't deserve it. His actions jeopardized his life and Tristan's. I agree with Tristan's decision that this was the only way to save his own life," Alistair stated.

"I respectfully disagree. There is no situation that allows for stealing another witch's magic. I believe the Clark magic needs to be returned to the Clarks," Penelope pronounced.

Morgan cleared her throat. "I agree with Penelope. We set a dangerous precedent, allowing magic to be stolen from a witch under any circumstance."

The pit at the bottom of my stomach morphed into the Grand Canyon as my gaze turned to Isaiah. "My vote goes with Alistair. Scott Clark lost his magic in the course of committing numerous crimes. Crimes that may result in the death penalty. In numerous states." Isaiah stated, looking bewildered at the women. To be honest, I was shocked at his vote. Hell, I was shocked at the women's votes. I became very worried. Common sense appeared to be severely lacking. I glanced at Kayla. She seemed slightly flabbergasted.

"Well, I guess the final vote belongs with me." Magna inhaled deeply. "I agree with the women. The magic needs to be returned to the Clark family."

A dead silence fell across the room for several moments. I couldn't breathe. I swallowed down my initial instinct to pull *Eadala* and start beheading idiots. I turned my murderous gaze on Kayla. She didn't look thrilled. She appeared horrified.

"I propose a vote of no confidence against the Board members." Someone stated from the middle of the gallery.

"I second the proposal." Stephen Kane announced, jumping to his feet.

"All those in favor?"

A resounding chorus of "Aye"s met the question.

"Those opposed?"

The only "Nay" responses came from the three women on the Board. I couldn't see who spoke and wasn't familiar enough with the other covens to identify the speaker making propositions.

"I propose Penelope, Magna and Morgan be removed."

"I second the proposal." Stephen stated.

"All those in favor?"

Another chorus of "Aye"s addressed the proposal.

"Those opposed?"

The three women responded weakly.

"So removed."

"Ladies, please move to the gallery," Alistair stated, smiling widely.

"I nominate Alberto Mendoza to fill one of the vacancies." Holy shit! I craned my neck trying to identify the speaker.

"I'll second that proposal." Once again, Stephen pronounced.

"All in favor?"

Uncle Al became the third board member.

"I nominate Alexandra Bishop."

"I second." She became the fourth member.

"I nominate Mary Clark." I announced. The room fell quiet.

Finally, Alistair stated, "You must be a coven leader or a second to nominate proposed board members."

Raising an eyebrow, I turned to Lance. "Wanna start sleeping again at night?"

Lance jumped up and stated, "I propose Mary Clark."

"Did she just threaten you?"

Lance laughed. "No. She just gave me a stay of execution. I haven't slept in days for fear of her retribution!"

"Why do you fear retribution?" Alistair questioned, glancing at me.

"I may have hit her with a sleep spell." Chuckles permeated the gallery.

"I second the proposal of Mary Clark as a Board member." Steve stated.

"All those in favor?"

A moment of silence fell across the room. Then, "Aye"s circled the room.

"All opposed?"

Again, the room fell silent. "New board members, take your seats." Alistair stated. Alberto, Alexandra and Mary sat at the table.

"I propose we vote on the matter of Tristan Mendoza and the Clark family magic." Alexandra stated.

"I second the proposal." Alistair stated. "All in favor of Tristan Mendoza keeping the Clark family magic after he was kidnapped by Scott Clark, held captive for six days without proper nourishment?"

The vote was unanimous.

"Now that common sense has finally returned to the Governing Board of Covens, can we address a few more items?" The unseen speaker asked.

A chorus of "Aye"s replied.

Completely flabbergasted, I turned to Lance. *What just happened? Our cousin's life got saved.*

Epilogue

𝕸onday Night Football found all the men from Salmon River Lodge at the Bitterroot River Clan Home and most of their women at ours. I manned the grill while Shay played tour guide. Everyone ordered rare steaks, except Eraina, the only non-Were in the house. She wanted hers burnt. The four unwilling guests of Scummy Ball Sack showed up, as well. Devon and I had spoken with them, offering the alternative of hanging out at the Salmon River Pride Home.

Dana and Chrissy stepped out on to the back patio. The perfect Indian Summer evening, the lodge provided shade from the sun. They helped themselves to drinks from the bar, as more women trickled out.

"Are those caves?" Dana asked, gazing at the canyon wall pock marked with openings.

I nodded. "Perfect dens, right in the backyard. Feel free to wander up and take a look. Only two are permanently occupied. Rhiannon and J-Dawg each chose a den." Rolling my eyes, "You'll be able to identify J-Dawg's 'crib' easily."

Chuckling, they followed the trail up and around, gazing into the caves. I heard their laughter on the breeze. J-Dawg insisted we refer to his den as a 'crib', the cool slang word. With the mentality of a twelve-year old, his decorating techniques reflected that. Using his light magic, colorful orbs brightened the dark interior. Posters of "hot female dragons" adorned the walls. He also began collecting treasure because, "Every dragon has a treasure trove!" His idea of treasure included anything sparkly or cool, including glitter fingernail polish and Happy Meal toys.

The four women retreated into the lodge and returned with blankets and pillows, each choosing a den. After their ordeal, sleeping in the open air, in their animal form provided them the most security, at the moment.

As they walked by us, Shay nudged me, knocking against my boob. I winced in pain. "What? Sex too rough?"

I shook my head. "There's no such thing." I rubbed the tender spot.

Unfortunately, Scummy Ball Sack healed from his injuries, thanks to his mom. Idaho charged him with the initial five homicides. It was determined that the victims were brought to his evil laboratory in Lewiston where he and his father killed them. Montana decided to wait and see what the outcome of the trial was prior to charging him with the four kidnappings, rape and torture. Oregon also chose to wait on Idaho before charging him with Eleanor's death.

Scott admitted Rosie died while he learned to teleport. He attempted to teleport her along with him. It didn't work. He lost control, ending up within the rock. He freaked out, dropping her, saving himself.

As for Kiki, he denied knowing her whereabouts. He stated he brought Carly, his first Montanan victim, home. Scott sent Kiki to the store to buy fresh raw meat, but she never returned. A couple days later, he found her car in Darby, parked at a bar. He drove it back to his house and never saw her again. Her cell phone had been left in the car.

Nez Perce County Sheriff's Department incarcerated Scott in a magic void cell. He received no physical contact with any visitor or inmate. Any and all items were inspected thoroughly before being passed on to him – whether it was legal papers from his attorney or a birthday card from his grandmother. The jail subjected his guards to intensive searches and monitoring. No chances for escape this time.

The next morning, I lay in my log bed, Malachi wrapped around me. A cool breeze blew through the open French doors. The roaring river lulling us to sleep. Consciousness slowly entered my mind. My stomach roiled.

I sprang to my feet, running to the bathroom. I barely made it to the toilet before tossing my steak from the night before. After puking my guts out, I reached for my toothbrush. My stomach roiled again. I opted for a very quick swish of mouthwash. I flushed the toilet and walked out onto my balcony, breathing deeply of the fresh air.

"You okay?" Malachi asked, sleepily from our bed.

"I don't know what the fuck that was," I focused on the breeze in my face.

"Are you pregnant?"

I laughed, "Only if divine intervention took place and the only god …" I hesitated, flashing back to the encounter with Mictlantcuhtli and his Goddess friend. "Oh, fuck!" I whispered.

Malachi decided to make an appearance at 3D Investigations since he hadn't been there in months. I tried to remember what Mictlantcuhtli called the goddess with his spear. Entering our library, I pulled out a book of deities. It seemed like her name started with an X or a Z. Xochiquetzal. That was her name!

I read the blurb about her. Son of a bitch! The goddess associated with fertility, beauty and female sexual power. Well, two out of three ain't bad. She considered marigolds sacred. Holy fuck!

Pulling my cell out of my pocket, I dialed a number. After several rings, my brother answered. "What?"

"Good morning. Where are you?"

"Uh," he hesitated, "Seattle it looks like."

"I need to talk to you."

He hesitated again, groaning, then moaning. "Gimme an hour and I'll meet you at your lodge."

"Why do you need an hour?"

"Because I'm not alone. Your men may not last long, but I make sure to please my women."

"TMI, brother!" I rolled my eyes. "Fine. One hour. At your cabin."

"Mmm. It's good to be king."

I hung up.

A little more than an hour later, I met Bane at the old miner's cabin. "What's up? Why did you want to meet here?"

I sighed. "I think I might be pregnant."

"Don't you know how to prevent that?" He asked, disdainfully.

"Yeah. I take herbs, birth control pills and I psionically control my hormones," I stated bitterly. I strongly believe in redundancy when it comes to birth control.

He raised an eyebrow, then placed a hand on my stomach. Bane held it there for several minutes. I tried to exercise all the patience I possessed. Sighing, he finally looked up at me. "You're pregnant. Do you have any idea how you got pregnant?"

"Mictlantecuhtli needed my assistance with obtaining his spear from an Aztec goddess named Xochiquezal. She required a sexual sacrifice before she returned his spear." Bane laughed, shaking his head as I explained. "She's the goddess of fertility."

Bane laughed, heartily. I stared at him, failing to find any part of this humorous. "What's so funny?" I asked belligerently.

"Well, it explains what's going on in your womb," he laughed, shaking his head, again.

Finding absolutely no humor in the situation, I screeched, "Bane! What the fuck is going on in my womb?"

"You're pregnant with triplets. Do you want to know the sexes or do one of those reveal things? We could have a reveal party! We could have three reveal parties!" He continued to laugh.

I punched him hard in the gut.

He held a hand up. "Alright, alright. Triplet boys. Human, not kittens. Here's the funny thing," he paused, I raised an eyebrow, waiting for the punchline. "There are three different dads. It appears your reproductive organs are that of a cat. Even though you're in human form and got pregnant in human form," he paused. "You got pregnant in human form, right?"

"Yes!" I snapped as I tried to wrap my mind around all of this. I wanted to kill Mictlantecuhtli.

"As I was saying, your reproductive organs are cat. Even though your babies are in human form, they're developing at the rate of kittens. The good news? You won't be pregnant for too long. Let me rephrase that. You won't be pregnant as long as a human female. But I'm going to need to monitor you. Between the Were and witch genes, I'm not sure how long you will be pregnant. We'll need to ensure the babies are fully developed prior to birth since they won't be hanging out as long as a human baby. I need to take a crash course on OB/GYN care of Weres and compare the developmental stages of your fetuses versus Were fetuses. Since you suffer from divine intervention, I would think everything will be fine. Don't suppose you could call Mickey or his lady friend?"

Mickey was the nickname Tristan bestowed upon Mictlantecuhtli.

I harrumphed. "Perhaps, if I prayed to them." I rolled my eyes.

"Well, at this point, everything looks good. How far along do you think you are?" Bane asked.

"About a week."

Bane looked completely surprised. "Wow. I don't know a whole lot yet about what to expect when you're expecting, but based on the developmental stage of the babies, I would have guessed a whole lot further along!"

I dropped my head, running a hand through my hair. What the hell do I do now? This was entirely my own fault. My Were-ness opened me up for multiple sexual encounters. Since I overindulged in birth control, I never even thought about my reproductive organs. It never occurred to me I couldn't trust Mictlantecuhtli. I sighed.

"Can I be a fly on the wall when you explain this to Malachi and Devon?"

I punched him again.